Enchanted River

Slumbering Wood

Fairy Village

Whistling Wood

Widdershins

Storehouse of Wishes

Magical Maze

Fairy Castle

Forget-me-not FAIRIES

hinkler

This book belongs to

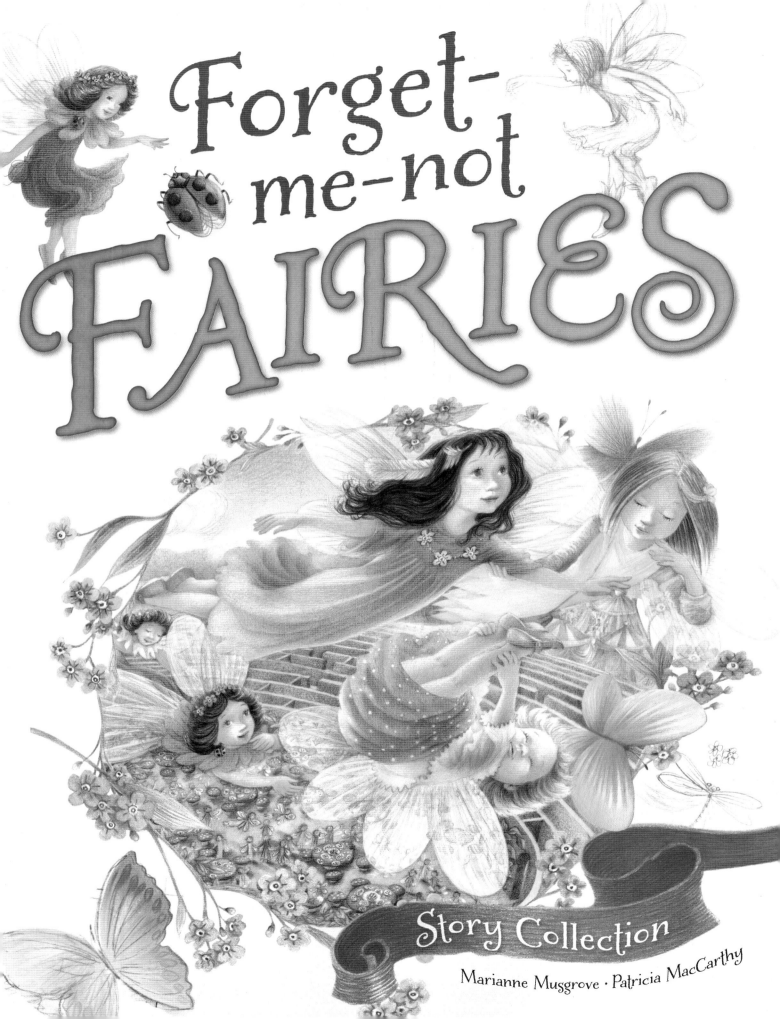

Forget-me-not FAIRIES

Story Collection

Marianne Musgrove · Patricia MacCarthy

Published by Hinkler Books Pty Ltd
45–55 Fairchild Street
Heatherton Victoria 3202 Australia
www.hinkler.com.au

hinkler

© Hinkler Books Pty Ltd 2013

Author: Marianne Musgrove
Lead Artist: Patricia MacCarthy
Art Director: Paul Scott
Senior Editor: Suzannah Pearce
Illustrators: Patricia MacCarthy, Jo Blake,
Catharine Collingridge and Jessica Johnson
Prepress: Graphic Print Group

www.mariannemusgrove.com.au
www.patriciamaccarthy.co.uk

Illustrations by:

Make a Wish: Patricia MacCarthy

The Naughty Fairy Princess: Catharine Collingridge

The Trouble with Teapots: Catharine Collingridge

The Fairy Queen's Birthday: Patricia MacCarthy

The Magic Ring of Toadstools: Patricia MacCarthy
and Jo Blake

Forget Me Not: Catharine Collingridge
and Jo Blake

Widdershins: Jessica Johnson and
Catharine Collingridge

Catch a Falling Star: Catharine Collingridge

The Fairies' Winter Ball: Patricia MacCarthy

The Lost Forest: Catharine Collingridge and
Jo Blake

Forever in Fairy Land: Patricia MacCarthy
and Jo Blake

ISBN 978 1 7430 8536 3

Printed and bound in China

Contents

The Wishing Song

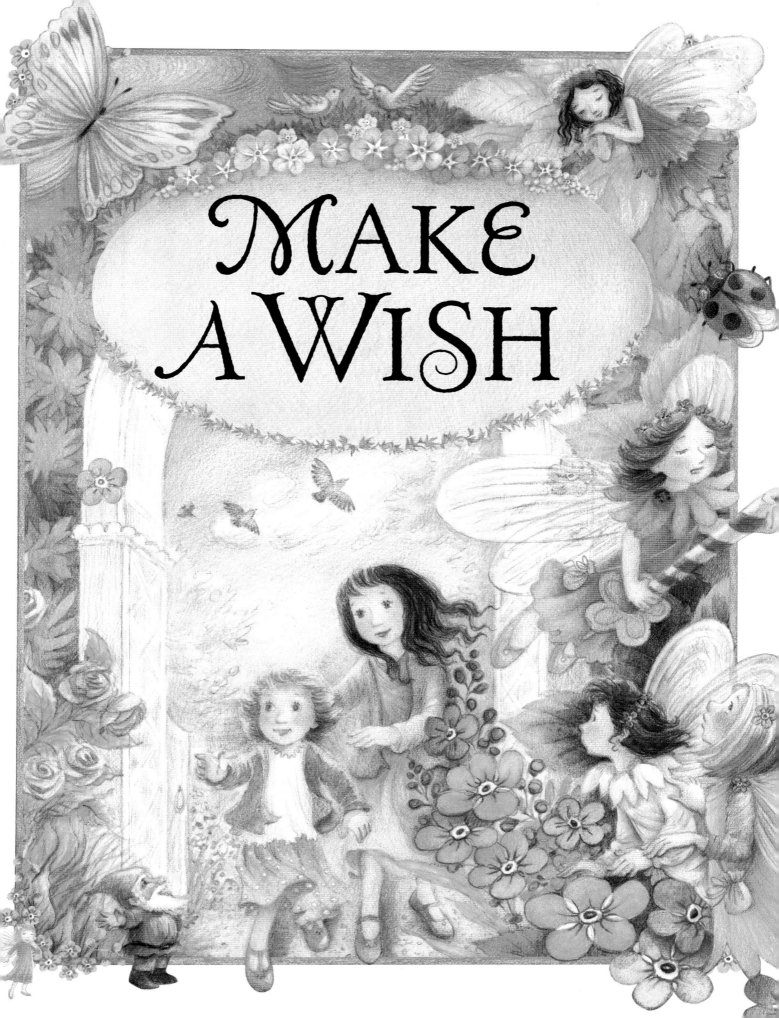

MAKE A WISH

'I can't believe they forgot my birthday!' said Sophie to her pet mouse, Scampers. A tear slid down her cheek and nestled in his fur.

Sophie and her family had moved to the country only a week ago, and everything was 'in an uproar' as Nora, the housekeeper, liked to say at least five times a day. Even so, thought Sophie, that was no excuse for forgetting. At least she had the treehouse to escape to.

'Little sis,' called Ellen. 'You up there? Mama needs you inside.'

Sophie climbed down the ladder, all the while wishing she were back in her old house with her old life and her old friends. She knew no one in the country, and she was miserable – simply miserable!

When Sophie walked into the sitting room, Mama, Papa, Ellen and Nora greeted her with a birthday cake topped with twinkling candles.

'Surprise!' they cried. 'Happy birthday!'

All at once, Sophie's sad tears turned to happy tears.

'Make a wish, darling,' said Mama.

'But don't tell us what it is or it won't come true,' added Ellen.

Knowing exactly what to wish for, Sophie took a deep breath and blew out her candles.

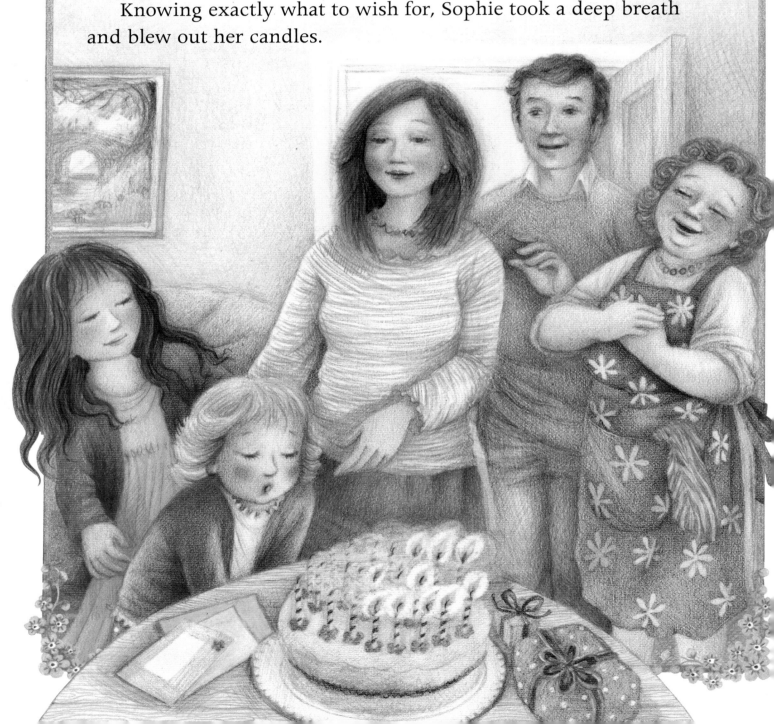

Later that day, Sophie slipped into the kitchen for another piece of cake. Ellen followed her, saying, 'Sophie, we're not supposed to eat more –'. Both girls froze. There, on the top of the cake, was a small winged creature trying to pull out a birthday candle.

'Come on, Zinny!' the creature muttered to herself. With one last tug, out came the candle. 'There! I *will* make a good wish fairy.'

'Fairy!' gasped Sophie.

Looking up, the creature squealed, took a deep breath and disappeared.

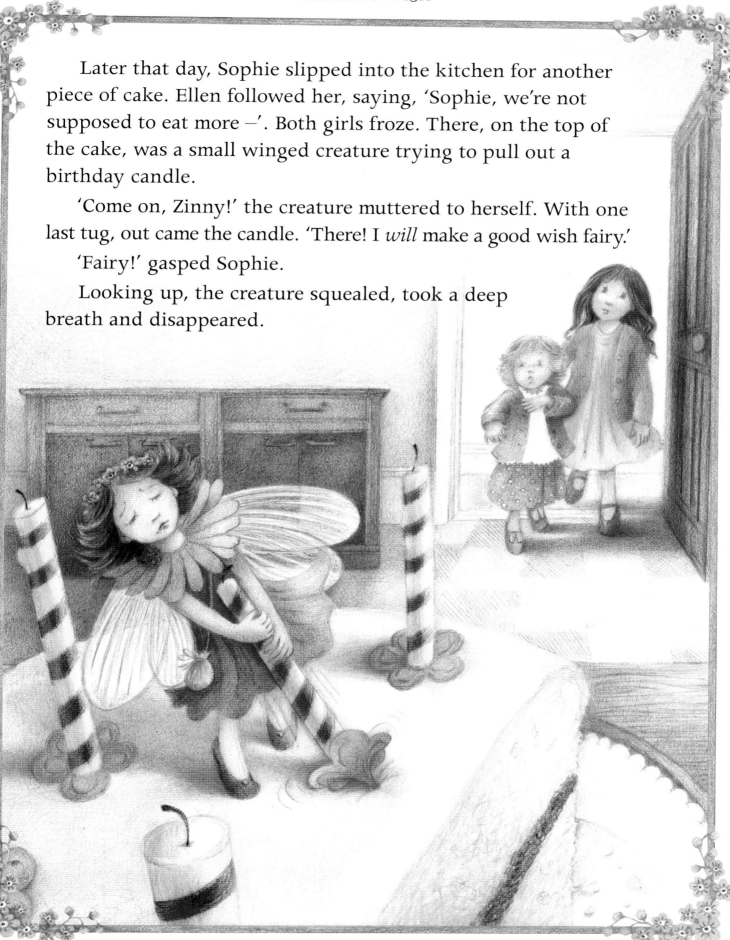

Zinny the fairy might have gone, but the candle had not. It floated out of the kitchen door and down the stone pathway. With eyes wide, the sisters followed. When they reached the back of the garden, the fairy reappeared. But, as soon as she spotted the girls, she took another breath and disappeared again. Then the gate opened by itself, and the candle floated through the gap and out of sight.

'Let's go too!' cried Sophie.

'But we're not allowed out of the garden – the woods aren't safe.'

Pouting, Sophie flopped down and leaned against what she thought was a rock, only to hear a voice cry, 'Careful!'. Sophie jumped up. It wasn't a rock at all, but a little garden gnome.

'You're alive!' cried Sophie.

'Well, of course I'm alive,' replied the gnome.

'B-but you're a statue,' stammered Ellen.

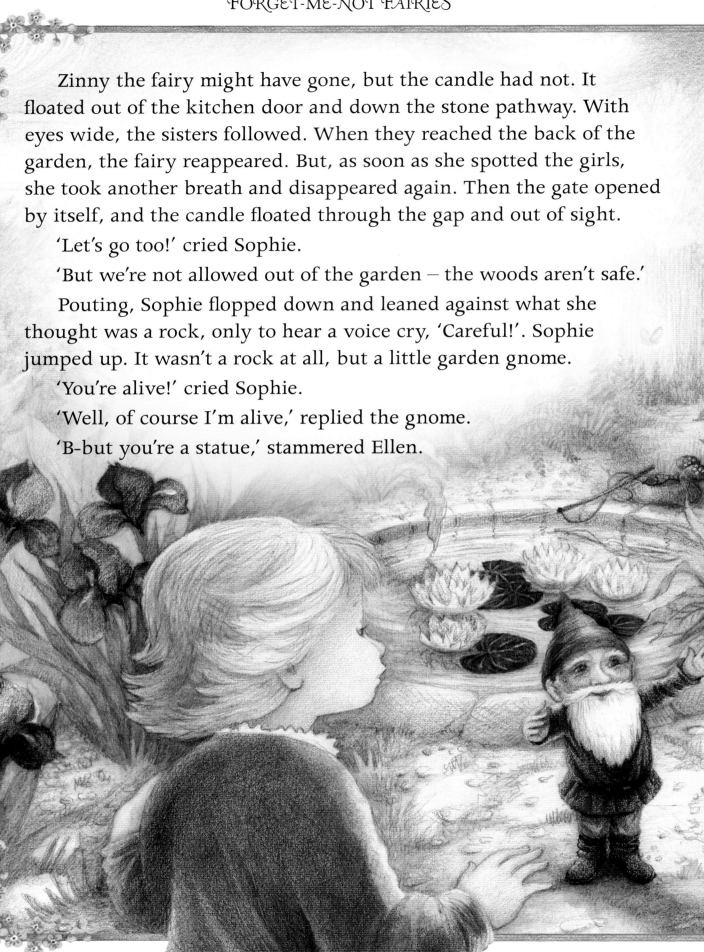

The gnome straightened his hat, and with as much
dignity as he could muster, said, 'Like all gnomes, I'm only
a statue when I choose to be.'

'What's your name?' asked Sophie.

'I'm Bilberry Grassblade Onionweed, keeper of the gate to
Wishaway Wood.'

The girls looked at each other in wonder. 'Wishaway Wood?'

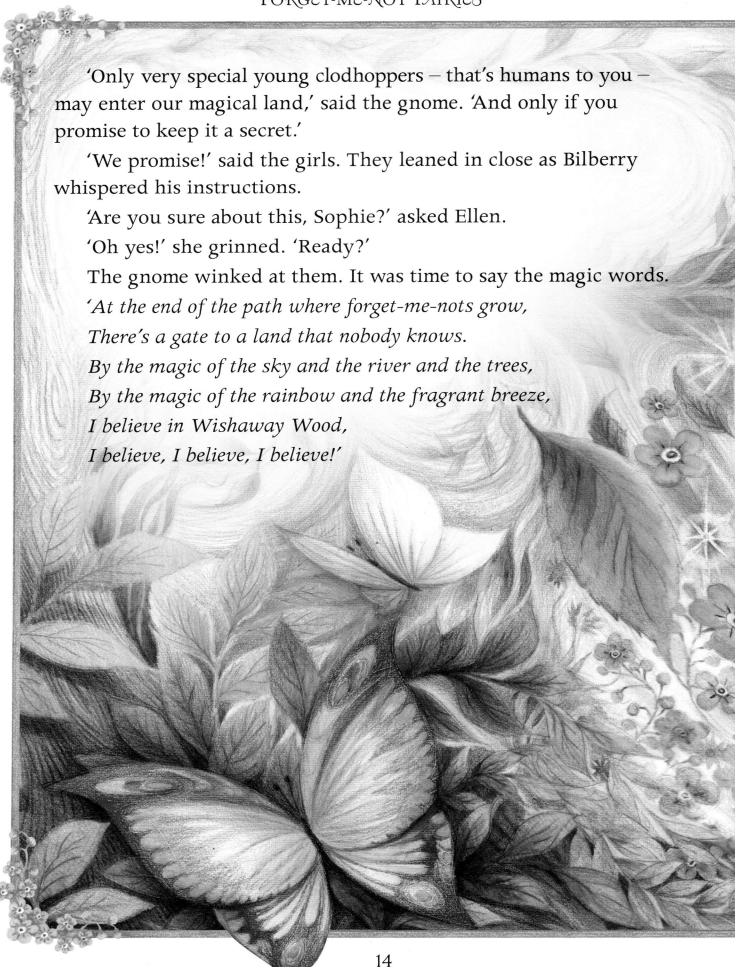

'Only very special young clodhoppers – that's humans to you – may enter our magical land,' said the gnome. 'And only if you promise to keep it a secret.'

'We promise!' said the girls. They leaned in close as Bilberry whispered his instructions.

'Are you sure about this, Sophie?' asked Ellen.

'Oh yes!' she grinned. 'Ready?'

The gnome winked at them. It was time to say the magic words.

'At the end of the path where forget-me-nots grow,
There's a gate to a land that nobody knows.
By the magic of the sky and the river and the trees,
By the magic of the rainbow and the fragrant breeze,
I believe in Wishaway Wood,
I believe, I believe, I believe!'

The girls turned anti-clockwise three times, then opened the gate and passed under the archway. All at once, wind rushed in their ears and there was beautiful music. They had a sense of falling upwards as lights shimmered and sparkled around them. Then, almost as soon as it began, everything stopped.

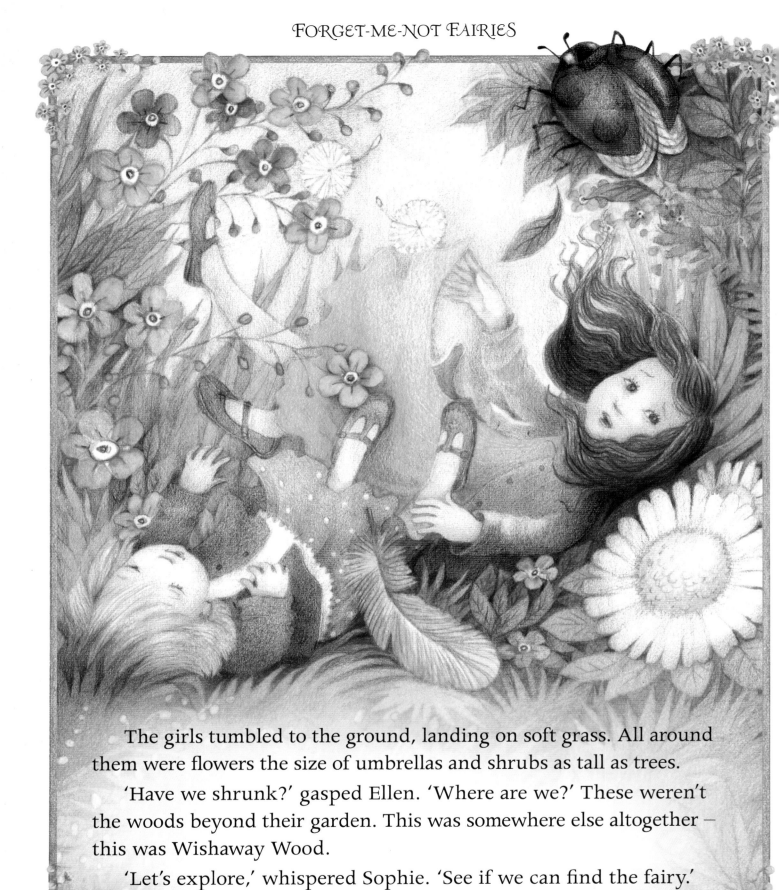

The girls tumbled to the ground, landing on soft grass. All around them were flowers the size of umbrellas and shrubs as tall as trees.

'Have we shrunk?' gasped Ellen. 'Where are we?' These weren't the woods beyond their garden. This was somewhere else altogether – this was Wishaway Wood.

'Let's explore,' whispered Sophie. 'See if we can find the fairy.'

Ellen gulped. 'All right.'

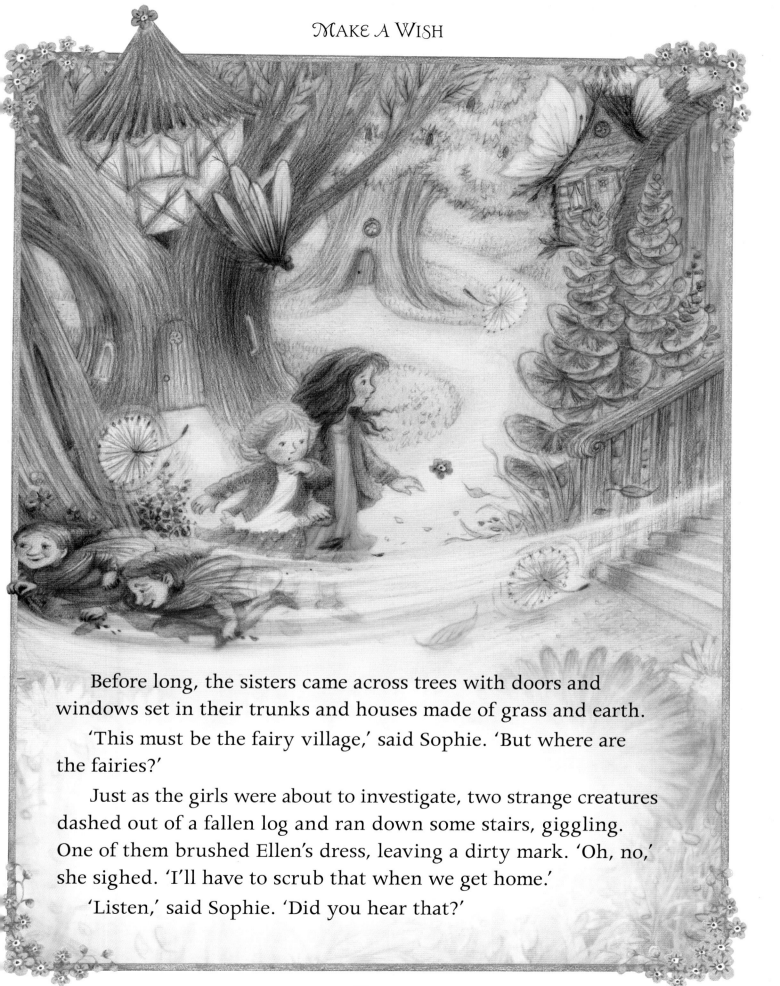

Before long, the sisters came across trees with doors and windows set in their trunks and houses made of grass and earth.

'This must be the fairy village,' said Sophie. 'But where are the fairies?'

Just as the girls were about to investigate, two strange creatures dashed out of a fallen log and ran down some stairs, giggling. One of them brushed Ellen's dress, leaving a dirty mark. 'Oh, no,' she sighed. 'I'll have to scrub that when we get home.'

'Listen,' said Sophie. 'Did you hear that?'

A sweet melody floated towards the sisters on the breeze. Holding hands, they followed the music until they came to a clearing. There, the girls found a group of fairies dancing and singing around a ring of toadstools. The little pink fairy they had seen before was among them, although the candle was nowhere in sight. The girls watched, mesmerised, as the fairies sang a song about granting wishes, called 'The Wishing Song'.

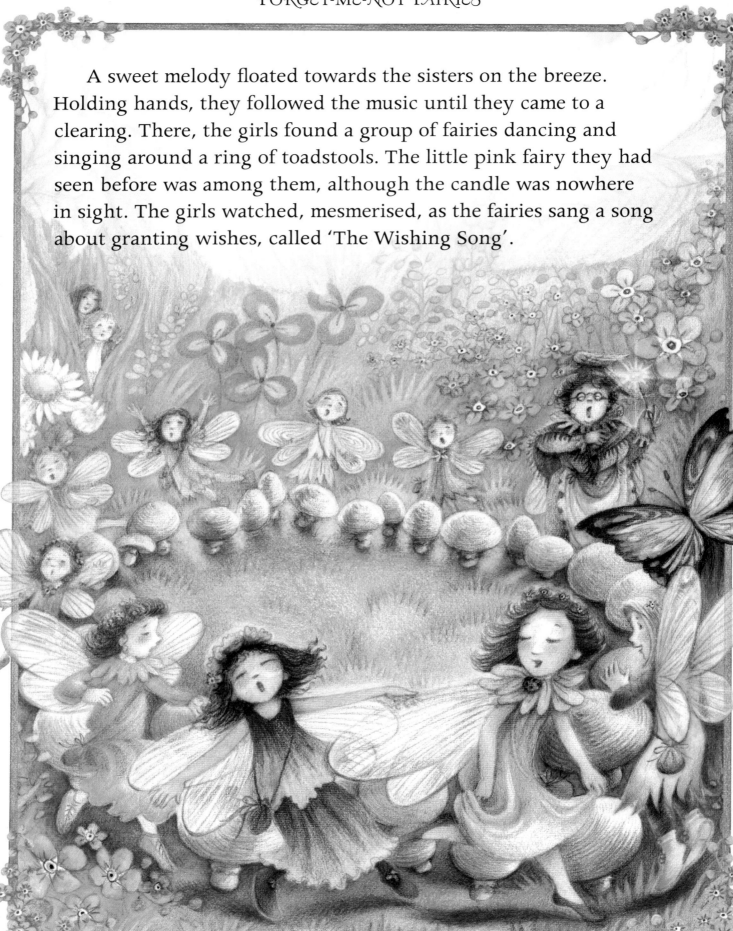

An older fairy with a pink and purple parrot on her shoulder raised her wand and declared in a loud voice: 'A kitten for Jane!'

A pool appeared in the centre of the toadstool ring, revealing an image of a girl being licked by a baby giraffe. The fairy peered at her wand, then back at the pool. The others stopped dancing.

'What happened, Mrs Milkthistle?' asked Zinny. 'That's meant to be a kitten, not a giraffe.'

'I know!' she replied. 'The question is not *what*, but *why*?'

Ellen and Sophie exchanged glances.

'To the Storehouse of Wishes!' cried Mrs Milkthistle. With that, she marched down the path, her parrot squawking in surprise.

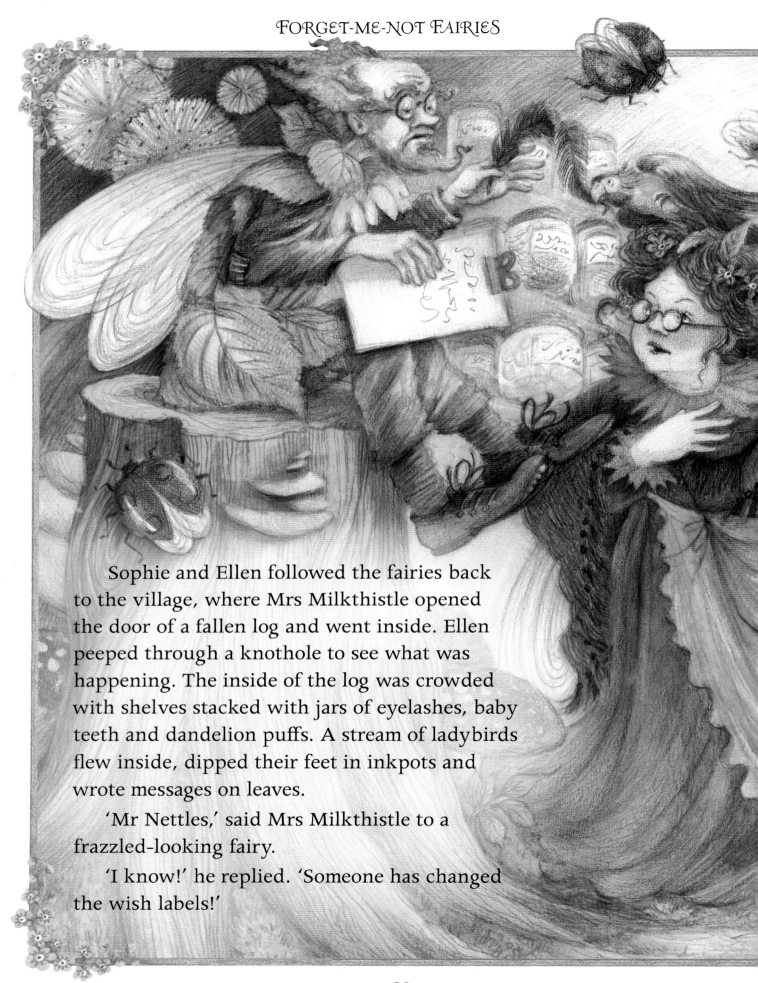

Sophie and Ellen followed the fairies back to the village, where Mrs Milkthistle opened the door of a fallen log and went inside. Ellen peeped through a knothole to see what was happening. The inside of the log was crowded with shelves stacked with jars of eyelashes, baby teeth and dandelion puffs. A stream of ladybirds flew inside, dipped their feet in inkpots and wrote messages on leaves.

'Mr Nettles,' said Mrs Milkthistle to a frazzled-looking fairy.

'I know!' he replied. 'Someone has changed the wish labels!'

It was Sophie's turn to look through the knothole.
As her eyes adjusted to the dim light, she spotted her
birthday candle with a label attached. She gasped loudly and
Mrs Milkthistle and Mr Nettles looked over.

'A clodhopper!' they cried.

The girls drew back, ready to make a run for it, but it was too late.

'They did it!' said one fairy.

'Meddlers!' cried another.

'We must take them to the Fairy Queen,' said Mrs Milkthistle,
emerging from the storehouse. 'Come,' she said to the girls, and
she hustled them down the path towards the woods.

After being poked and prodded by some very cross fairies, the girls arrived at a grand tree standing in the woods. It had a vast entrance in the trunk, and its branches stretched to the sky. It seemed to pulse with life.

'We are here to see Queen Flora,' said Mrs Milkthistle to a guard. 'The matter is urgent.'

Ellen and Sophie glanced at each other nervously.

'Don't worry, Sophie,' whispered a voice.

Sophie looked around to see who had spoken. It was Zinny, the little pink fairy who had stolen her candle.

'How do you know my name?' she whispered back. Before Zinny could answer, the guard ushered everyone into the tree.

Ellen and Sophie were led up and down winding staircases until they came to a throne room. There, before them, sat the Fairy Queen wearing a crown that glittered like a starburst. This was not just any tree, the girls realised. It was a fairy castle!

Mrs Milkthistle curtsied to the queen, then whispered to her. Queen Flora waved for the girls to step forward. Although beautiful, her eyes were serious. 'As queen of this land, I send my fairies into the world to collect the wishes of clodhoppers such as yourselves. It is our purpose to make those wishes come true.'

So that was why Zinny took my birthday candle, thought Sophie.

'Because you changed the wish labels,' continued the queen, 'there are some very disappointed clodhoppers in the world today. I'm afraid such serious wrong-doing cannot go unpunished.'

Punishment? Sophie's heart beat faster. She hoped there wasn't a dungeon in the castle. 'We didn't do it!' she cried.

Mutters of disbelief echoed around the room, before a little voice piped up. 'I'm sure they're innocent.' It was Zinny.

'Then they must prove it,' said the queen.

Yes, thought Ellen, *but how*?

Ellen looked down and saw the dirty mark on her dress. 'I know who did it!' she cried. 'When we first got here, Sophie and I saw some creatures running out of the Storehouse of Wishes. You keep ink in there, don't you? One of the creatures touched my dress – and look!'

Zinny came forward and peered at the mark. 'It's a pixie handprint!' she said. 'In ink! *They* changed the labels!'

The room erupted as fairies surrounded the girls, crying: 'The pixies did it! The mystery is solved! Hurrah for the clodhoppers!'

The girls hugged. They weren't going to the dungeon after all!

'Sophie and Ellen,' said Queen Flora, holding up a hand for silence. 'It seems we have misjudged you. Please accept my humble apologies. You deserve our thanks.' She took a handful of fairy dust and threw it into the air. Suddenly, there appeared two forget-me-not flower chains in her lap. 'Come here.'

Trembling with relief, Sophie and Ellen stepped forward. As the queen placed the chains over their heads, she said, 'These tokens will allow you to enter Wishaway Wood whenever you choose.'

Sophie and Ellen looked at each other and beamed.

'But,' added Queen Flora, 'if you ever take them off, you will forget everything you ever saw. And should you stay longer than one day and one night, you will be unable to return home and must remain here forever. Do you understand?'

Sophie and Ellen nodded. They could easily remember that. The most important thing was that they could come back!

When the fairies escorted the girls back to the entrance of Wishaway Wood, Zinny took their hands. 'Until next time,' she said. 'Oh, and Sophie, we haven't forgotten your birthday wish.'

'Goodbye,' said Ellen and Sophie. With that, the sisters stepped through the archway. When they arrived on the other side, they had returned to their normal size.

Later that day, the girls were in their bedroom recounting their adventures. 'You know what, Ellen?' said Sophie, touching the forget-me-not chain around her neck, 'I think I might like living in the country after all.'

'And has your birthday wish come true, little sis?'

'Oh yes. I wished –'

'Girls, where are you?' called Mama.

'Wished for what?' asked Ellen.

'To be invisible for a day!' finished Sophie. She took a deep breath and disappeared just as Mama entered the room.

'Where's Sophie? Oh, never mind, Ellen, you'll do. Nora needs some help with the dishes.'

Ellen pursed her lips together. Trust Sophie!

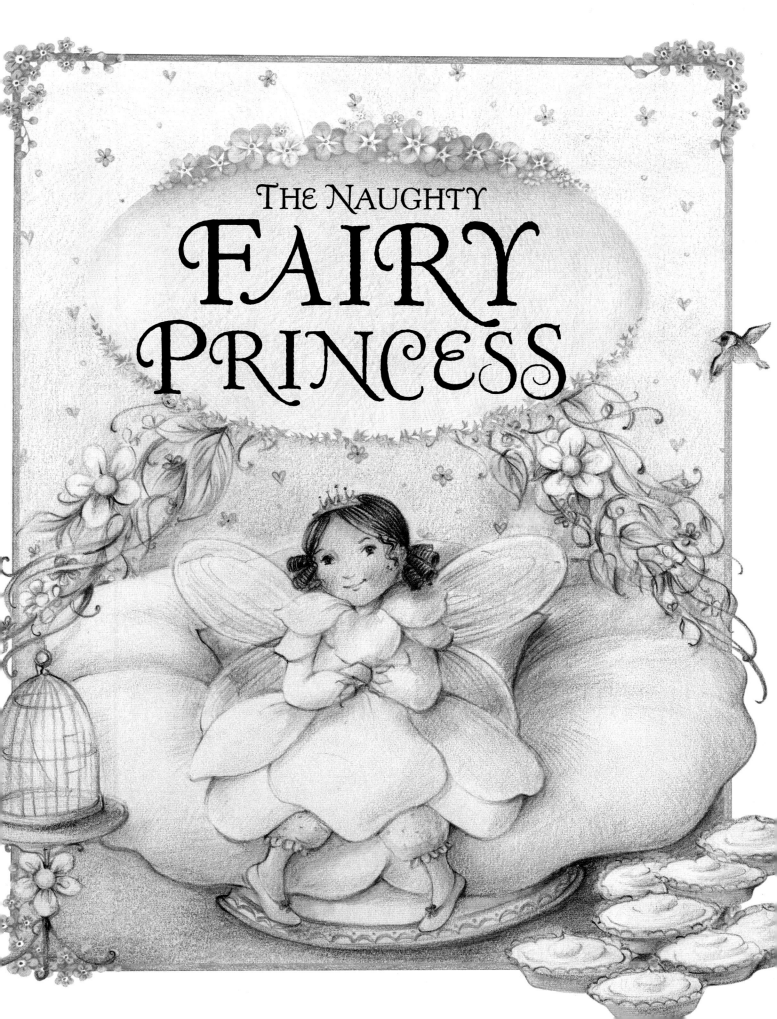

THE NAUGHTY
FAIRY PRINCESS

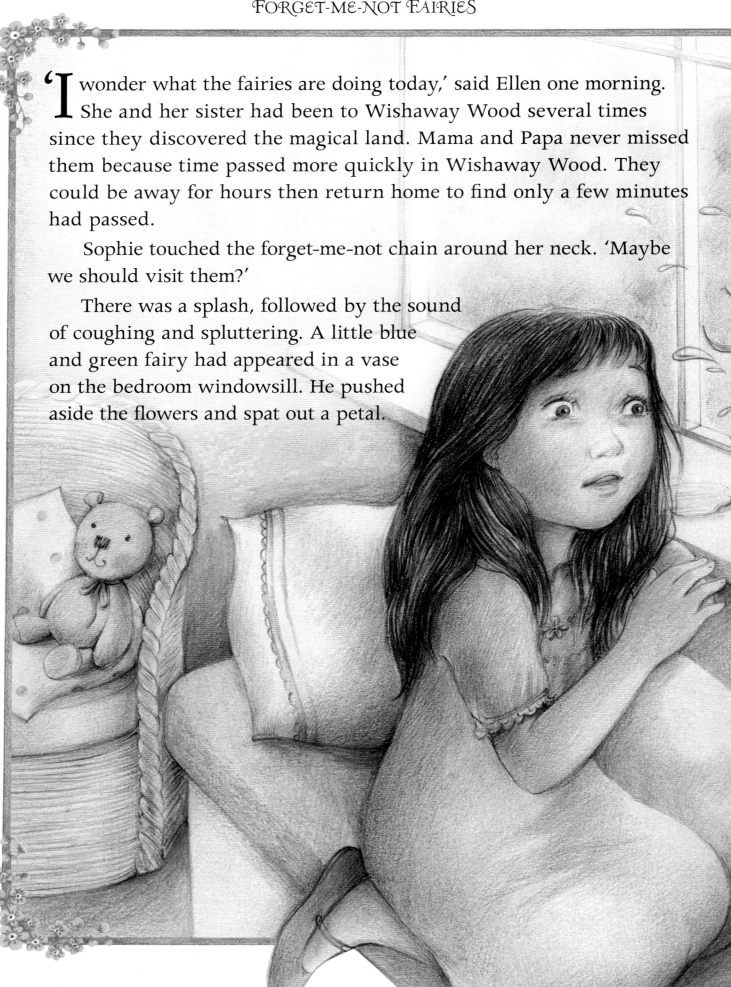

'I wonder what the fairies are doing today,' said Ellen one morning. She and her sister had been to Wishaway Wood several times since they discovered the magical land. Mama and Papa never missed them because time passed more quickly in Wishaway Wood. They could be away for hours then return home to find only a few minutes had passed.

Sophie touched the forget-me-not chain around her neck. 'Maybe we should visit them?'

There was a splash, followed by the sound of coughing and spluttering. A little blue and green fairy had appeared in a vase on the bedroom windowsill. He pushed aside the flowers and spat out a petal.

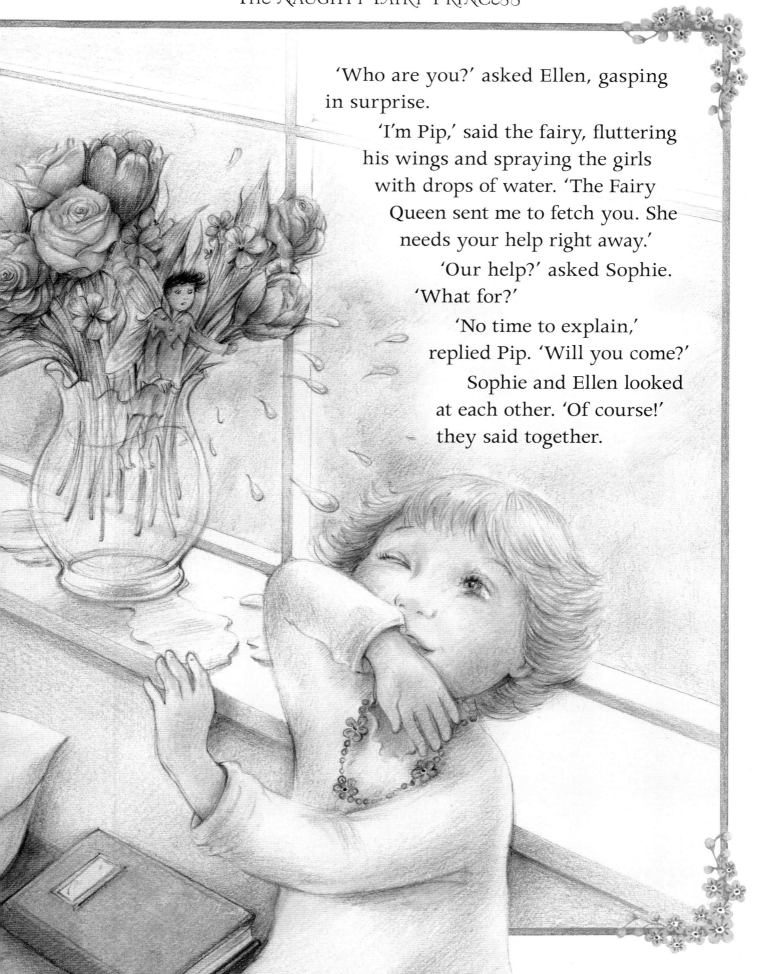

'Who are you?' asked Ellen, gasping in surprise.

'I'm Pip,' said the fairy, fluttering his wings and spraying the girls with drops of water. 'The Fairy Queen sent me to fetch you. She needs your help right away.'

'Our help?' asked Sophie. 'What for?'

'No time to explain,' replied Pip. 'Will you come?'

Sophie and Ellen looked at each other. 'Of course!' they said together.

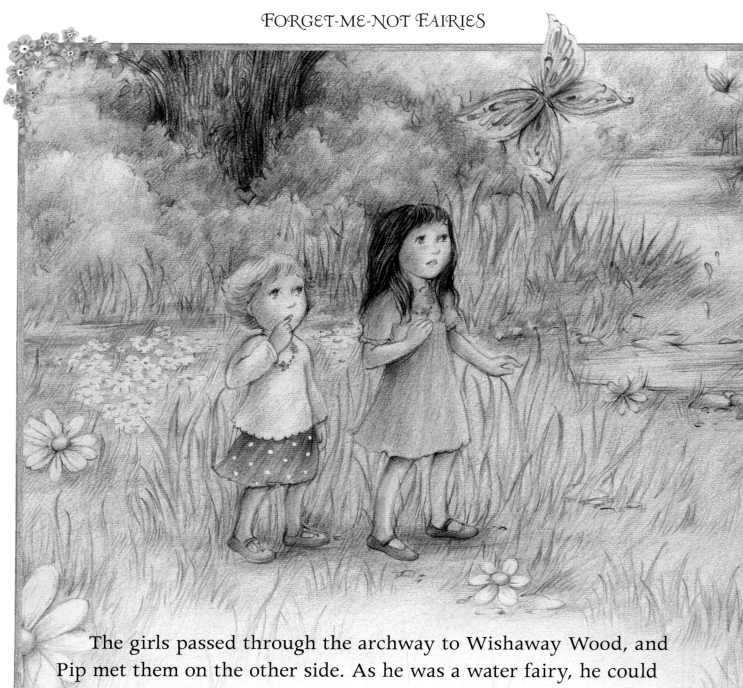

The girls passed through the archway to Wishaway Wood, and Pip met them on the other side. As he was a water fairy, he could travel by popping up in puddles and ponds along the way.

'The Fairy Castle is that way,' he said pointing down the path. Then he jumped into a puddle and popped up in another one further along. 'Come on!' he beckoned.

When the little group arrived at the castle, Pip looked around nervously. 'I have to go now,' he said. 'Good luck!' Then he dived into a pool of water and disappeared.

'Why would we need luck?' asked Sophie.

At that moment, a fairy flew out of the castle, waving her arms and shrieking, 'I can't take it anymore!'

'Can we help you?' asked Ellen.

The fairy stopped and stared at them, her face and clothes covered in cream pie. 'The princess keeps conjuring pies and throwing them at me!' she cried.

'She does?' said Sophie.

'Yes!' replied the fairy, wiping cream out of her eyes. 'Last week, she turned my hair green. The week before that, she cast a spell and I grew a squirrel's tail. They'll have to find another nanny. I quit!' With that, she flew off into the forest.

'Goodness!' said Ellen. 'I hope we don't have to meet this Fairy Princess.'

The girls were shown into the throne room, where the Fairy Queen was holding her head in her hands.

'Thank you for coming,' said Queen Flora. 'I'm at my wits' end! The princess has locked herself in her bedroom. Whenever I send someone to fetch her, she throws a cream pie at them!'

'But how can we help?' asked Sophie.

'You can find out what's wrong with her,' said the queen. 'She loves clodhoppers, you see. She's read all about your kind. She'll talk to you.'

Ellen and Sophie glanced at each other nervously. 'I suppose we can try,' said Ellen, thinking of the pie-covered nanny. Secretly, she wished she had worn old clothes.

A fairy took the girls down a winding staircase to the princess's bedroom. She knocked softly on the door, and then ran and hid behind Ellen.

'Go away!' a voice replied. 'Or else!'

'Please, Princess,' said the fairy, 'two clodhoppers are here to visit you.'

The door opened a crack, and the princess peeked out. 'Did you say clodhoppers?'

Princess Primrose showed the girls into her bedroom. Vines grew down from the ceiling, encircling a bed made of a giant flower. A tiny goldfinch zoomed around the room.

'Do sit down, clodhoppers,' said the princess, clasping her hands with excitement. She stamped her foot twice, and two toadstools appeared.

The girls sat down, nervously eyeing off a stack of cream pies.

'I'm so happy you came,' said the princess. 'You must tell me all about your land – about lemonade, lawnmowers, haircuts, bicycles, everything!'

'I have a bicycle,' said Sophie.

'Could I ride it?' asked the princess, eagerly. Then her face fell, and she slumped on her bed. 'Oh, but I'm not allowed out of the castle. It's so unfair! Goldie is my only friend.' She waved at the little goldfinch, who flew over and perched on her finger.

'Is that why you throw cream pies at everyone?' asked Ellen. 'Because you're lonely and bored?'

Princess Primrose shrugged sadly, and Sophie and Ellen felt sorry for her.

'What if we ask the queen if you could come to our house for a sleepover?' suggested Sophie.

'A sleepover!' cried the princess, her eyes lighting up. 'Yes, please!'

After the queen agreed, Sophie, Ellen and Princess Primrose went by carriage across Wishaway Wood. They stepped through the archway and tumbled into the Land of the Clodhoppers. The sisters had returned to their normal size, but the princess was still small.

'Welcome back,' said Bilberry, the gnome. He bowed and doffed his hat to the princess. The princess nodded.

'Hello, Bilberry,' said the girls.

Princess Primrose flew up onto Ellen's hand. 'Now, remember,' said Ellen, 'it's important to keep out of sight of grown-ups.'

'Yes,' said the princess, but she was not listening. 'Oooh, a bicycle!' And she flew off before the girls could stop her.

'Better hurry after her,' said Bilberry. 'I hear from her nanny she's a handful.'

For the rest of the day, Princess Primrose dashed from place to place, unable to contain her excitement. After a day of running after her and distracting the grown-ups, the girls were exhausted!

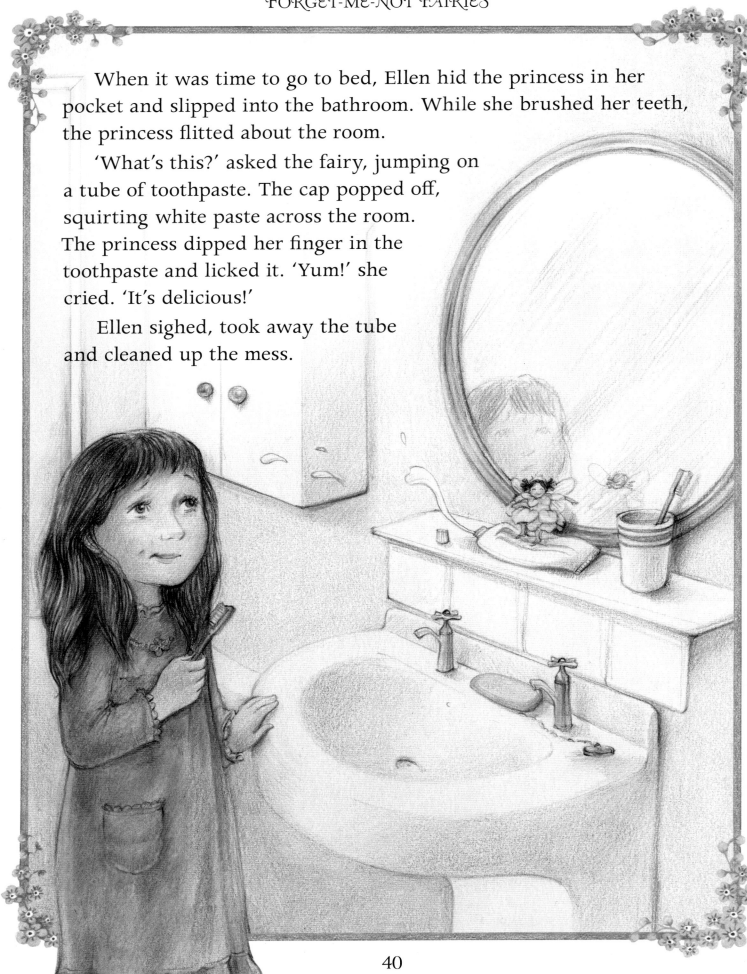

When it was time to go to bed, Ellen hid the princess in her pocket and slipped into the bathroom. While she brushed her teeth, the princess flitted about the room.

'What's this?' asked the fairy, jumping on a tube of toothpaste. The cap popped off, squirting white paste across the room. The princess dipped her finger in the toothpaste and licked it. 'Yum!' she cried. 'It's delicious!'

Ellen sighed, took away the tube and cleaned up the mess.

Sophie made Princess Primrose a bed out of a shoebox and some handkerchiefs. When the princess saw it, she clapped her hands and dived in. 'I've never been on a sleepover before!' she said. 'It's so nice to have friends.'

Ellen and Sophie smiled at her, and then climbed into bed themselves.

''Night, 'night,' said Sophie. 'Sleep tight, Primrose.'

When Princess Primrose didn't reply, Sophie peeked into the shoebox. The princess was fast asleep, snoring gently.

The next day, the sisters played in the garden with Princess Primrose. It was not long before Pip popped up in the birdbath, much to the princess's disappointment.

'Time to go home, Princess,' said Pip. 'Your carriage awaits you on the other side of the archway.'

'I can't possibly leave,' said Princess Primrose, crossing her arms. 'I'm having far too much fun!'

Pip glanced at the girls and sighed deeply. 'Please, Princess, you must.'

'Why?' she argued. 'No one would miss me. Anyway, you can't make me!' Then she flew up into the treehouse and conjured a cream pie.

'Oh, no,' groaned Sophie and Ellen.

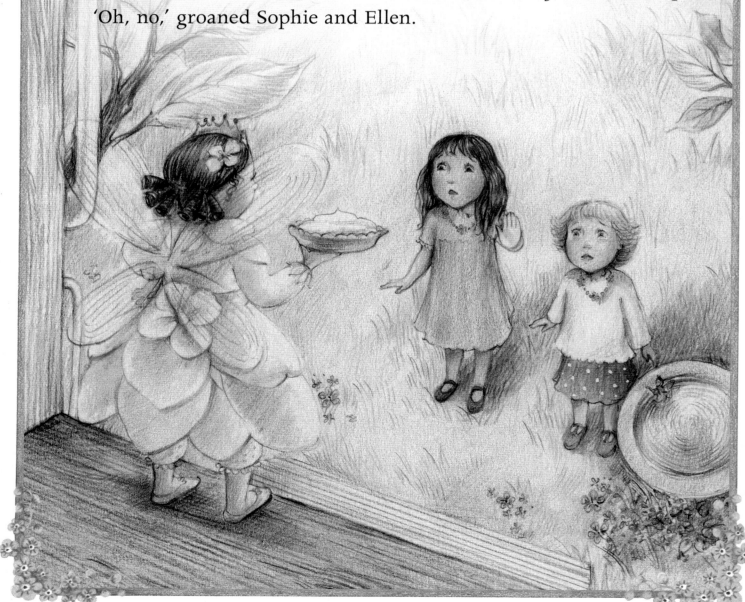

Pip sighed again, but Sophie had an idea. She whispered
something in Pip's ear, and he brightened up. 'Step back,' he said
to the girls, and he cast a spell. A ball of mist appeared in the air.
Inside it was an image of a goldfinch chirruping sadly.

'That's Goldie!' said Princess Primrose. 'Why does he look so sad?'

'Because he misses you,' answered Sophie. 'If you never go home,
he'll be ever so lonely.'

'Poor Goldie!' the princess said, laying down her pie. 'All right,
I'll go. But only if you promise to visit soon.'

'We promise!' replied Ellen, grinning at Sophie. 'You couldn't
keep us away.'

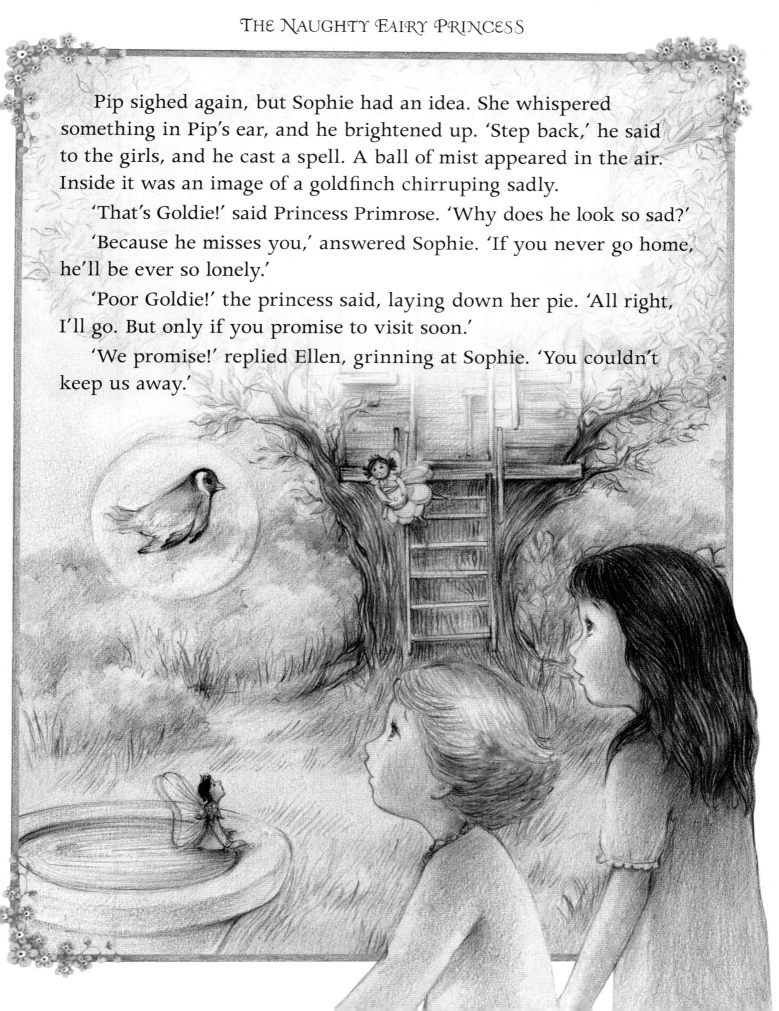

Not long after, the sisters went to Wishaway Wood for a picnic with the princess.

'Guess what, Primrose?' said Sophie. 'We just talked to the queen, and she's agreed to let you go to Fairy School! You'll have friends!'

'Thank you!' cried the princess, clapping her hands.

'We also brought you a gift,' said Ellen.

'Toothpaste!' cried the princess. 'Yum!' She dipped in her spoon.

'No, wait!' said Ellen, laughing. 'It's to clean your teeth with, not to eat.'

Princess Primrose raised an eyebrow. 'How funny you clodhoppers are! You must visit me again and share more of your strange customs.'

'We'd love to,' said the girls. And so they did.

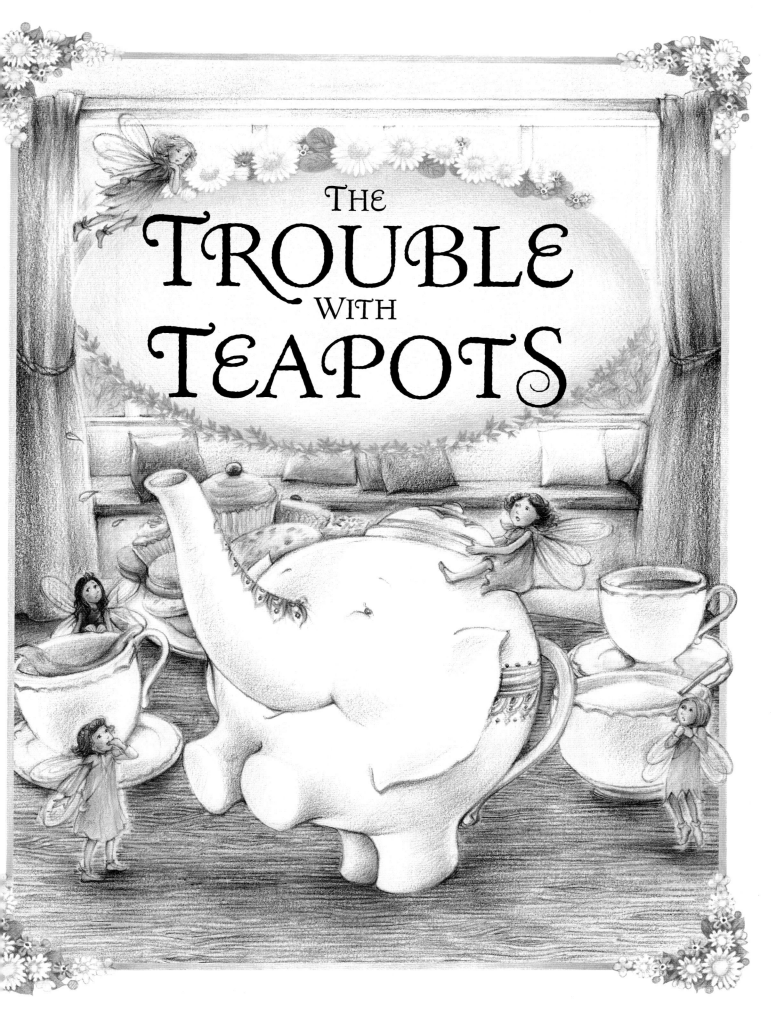

The
TROUBLE
WITH
TEAPOTS

'Ellen, have you seen Scampers?' asked Sophie one morning. 'I've searched everywhere.'

'I thought Mama said he wasn't allowed out of his cage,' said Ellen, putting away some plates for Nora.

'Yes, but he gets lonely,' replied Sophie. 'And he – uh oh!' High up on the sideboard, Sophie spotted her mouse. 'Scampers! Come down!'

The mouse twitched his whiskers as if to say, 'But I'm having so much fun up here.'

Sophie hauled herself up onto the ledge and reached out to her pet.

'Careful, little sis,' said Ellen, biting her thumbnail. 'Don't fall!'

Just as Sophie was about to scoop up Scampers, her foot slipped and she knocked over Mama's special elephant-shaped teapot. Ellen lunged forward to catch it, but she was too late. *Crash!* The teapot landed on the floor, and the spout broke off.

'Oh, no!' cried Sophie.

'It's worse than that,' said Ellen. 'Mama wants to use it for this afternoon's tea party.'

'What am I going to do?'

Ellen thought for a moment. 'Maybe the fairies can help?'

Sophie stowed the teapot in her bag, and then she and Ellen went to Wishaway Wood.

As soon as the girls found Zinny, they explained their problem. 'Don't worry,' said Zinny. 'Mrs Milkthistle will know what to do.' She pointed to the cottage with a butterfly on its roof, and over they went to ask for help.

Much to the girls' surprise, the door knocker blew a raspberry at them. Then the cottage stood up and did a little jig.

'It has legs!' cried Ellen. 'It's dancing!'

'That's because she's happy to see you,' said Mrs Milkthistle, poking her head out of a window. 'Welcome to "Widdershins"!'

After the cottage had finished its jig, it sat back down and allowed the girls inside.

'Hmmm,' said Mrs Milkthistle, turning over the broken teapot. 'I've just the thing. But first, you must put on a raincoat and hat. You never know what you'll find in the magic cupboard – fireworks, flying pigs, a river of chocolate ...'

Secretly hoping it was a river of chocolate, Sophie reached for the hatstand. It bowed to her and offered her its coats and hats. As she and Ellen dressed, Mrs Milkthistle opened an umbrella.

'Ready, petals?' said the fairy, bracing herself. Then she opened the cupboard door, and out blew a snowstorm.

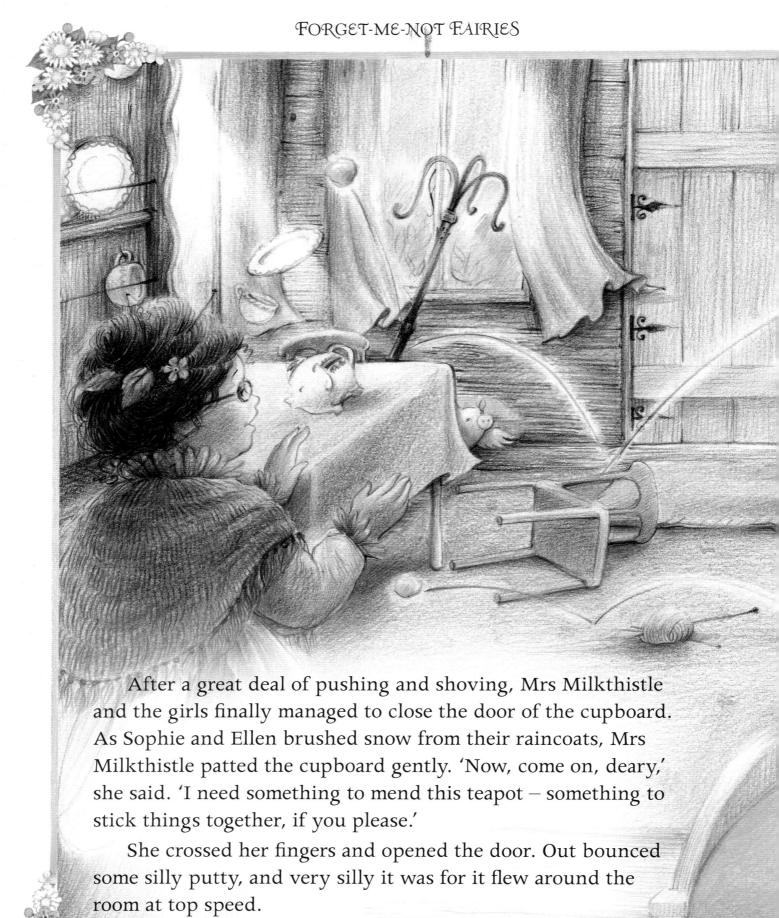

After a great deal of pushing and shoving, Mrs Milkthistle and the girls finally managed to close the door of the cupboard. As Sophie and Ellen brushed snow from their raincoats, Mrs Milkthistle patted the cupboard gently. 'Now, come on, deary,' she said. 'I need something to mend this teapot – something to stick things together, if you please.'

She crossed her fingers and opened the door. Out bounced some silly putty, and very silly it was for it flew around the room at top speed.

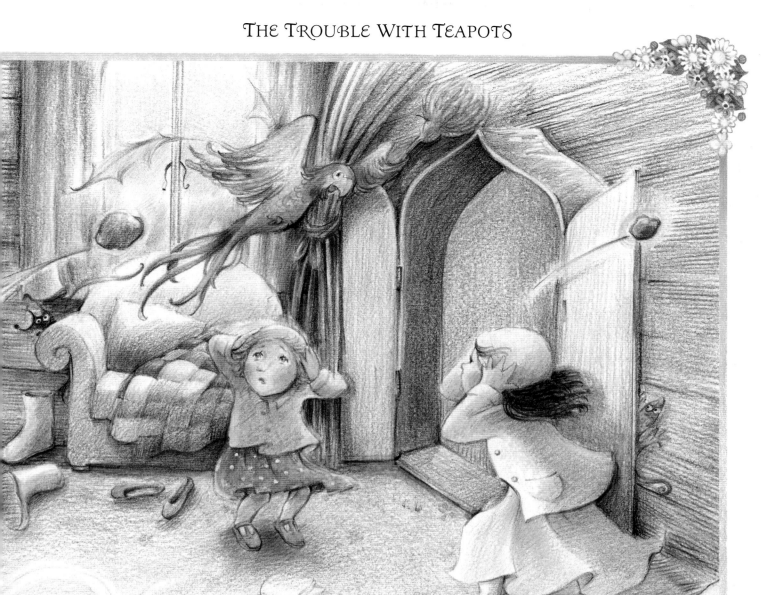

'Duck!' cried Mrs Milkthistle, as a particularly large blob sailed over their heads.

Sophie and Ellen took cover while the fairy's pink and purple parrot flew in circles, squawking.

'Don't worry, petals,' said Mrs Milkthistle. She took a handful of fairy dust and blew on it. Out of nowhere, a large velvet bag appeared, which she used to capture all the putty. 'There,' she said, tying up the bag and wrestling it back into the cupboard. 'That's one problem solved.'

Unfortunately, the teapot was still broken.

Sighing softly, Mrs Milkthistle flopped onto her chair. 'What's this?' she said, picking up a jar. 'Why, it's magic glue! I wonder where that came from.'

Little did she know, the glue had been put there by some tricksy pixies, who wanted to make mischief.

Mrs Milkthistle unscrewed the lid and began mending the teapot. When it was done, Sophie put it in her bag. 'Thank you so much,' she said.

'You're most welcome,' Mrs Milkthistle replied.

'And, now, we'd better get going,' said Ellen. 'We have to get back for Mama's tea party.'

Zinny and her friends escorted the sisters back to the gateway between Wishaway Wood and The Land of the Clodhoppers (or 'home', as Sophie and Ellen liked to call it).

No one noticed the little elephant teapot peeking out of Sophie's bag, a playful glint in its eye.

When the girls got home, the guests had already arrived. Sophie quickly returned the teapot to the sideboard in the hallway, and she and Ellen went into the sitting room.

'There you are, girls!' said Mama. 'Mrs Harwood was just about to play a tune for us.'

While the grown-ups gathered around the piano, Nora brought in the tea things. As Nora was leaving, Sophie turned around and almost fainted. The elephant teapot was leaning over the sweet plate, sniffing. It was alive! And what's more, it was about to eat their afternoon tea! 'Goodness!' she cried, and she rushed over to snatch a cupcake from its mouth.

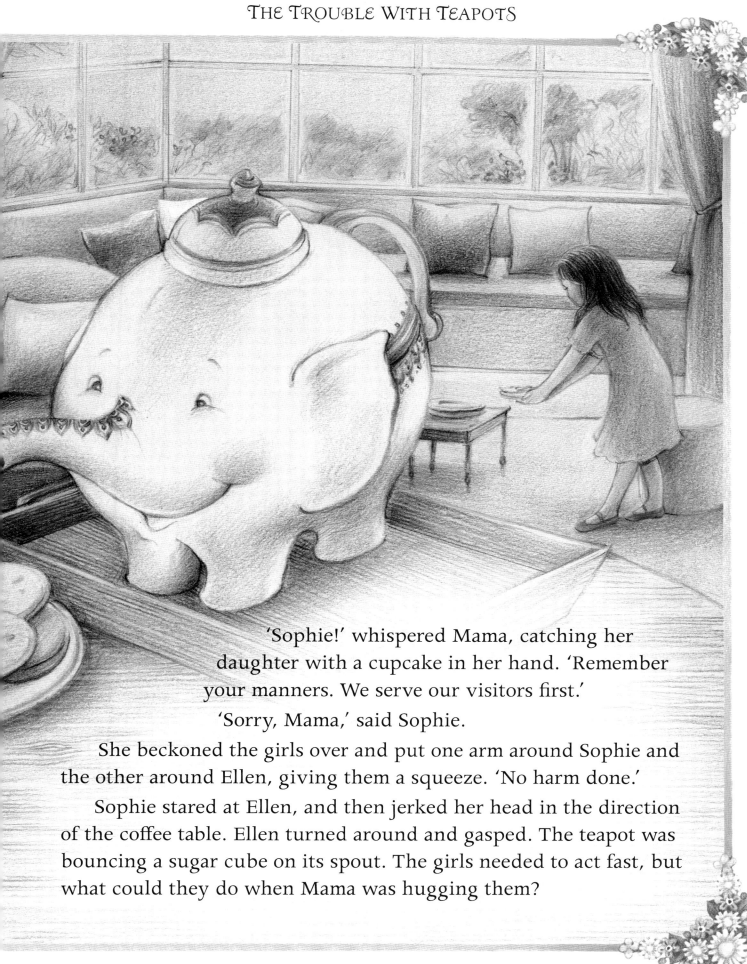

'Sophie!' whispered Mama, catching her daughter with a cupcake in her hand. 'Remember your manners. We serve our visitors first.'

'Sorry, Mama,' said Sophie.

She beckoned the girls over and put one arm around Sophie and the other around Ellen, giving them a squeeze. 'No harm done.'

Sophie stared at Ellen, and then jerked her head in the direction of the coffee table. Ellen turned around and gasped. The teapot was bouncing a sugar cube on its spout. The girls needed to act fast, but what could they do when Mama was hugging them?

Reading each other's minds, the girls touched their forget-me-not chains and made a wish. *Come to us, fairies. We need your help!*

Sophie risked a quick peek over her shoulder. The teapot was doing a handstand. *Oh no!* Any moment now, Mrs Harwood would finish her song and they would be discovered. *Come on, Zinny!*

As their guest played the final notes, there was a loud crash from the corner of the room. A pot plant had tipped over, seemingly by itself, but actually at the hands of fairies Willow, Poppy and Snowdrop – the perfect distraction!

'Dear me!' said Mama, going over to investigate.

While the rest of the grown-ups followed her, the sisters turned to find Zinny hovering above the coffee table. The teapot had just finished guzzling all the milk from the milk jug and was drawing back its spout, ready to spray milky tea all over the room. Zinny threw a handful of fairy dust into the air, and a stopper appeared. She tossed it to Ellen, who popped it in the elephant's spout. Then Zinny jumped on the teapot's back and tried to calm it down. Instead, it pranced around the coffee table, doing circus tricks.

'Steady, girl!' whispered Zinny.

It was not long before the teapot had had enough of the stopper. It puffed out its cheeks and blew it into the air, along with a stream of milky tea. Sophie grabbed the empty milk jug and caught it just in time. A moment later, the grown-ups turned around.

'What are you doing with the milk jug, darling?' asked Mama.

'It's, ah, dusty,' said Sophie, making sure to block the view of the coffee table.

'It is?' said Mama. 'I thought Nora had cleaned everything.'

'I-I was supposed to,' stammered Ellen, standing next to Sophie. 'Sorry, I forgot.'

'Whoa there!' whispered Zinny behind them.

The girls inched even closer.

'Why don't I take everything out to the kitchen?' offered Ellen. 'I can ask Nora to bring out the other set.'

'I'll help!' said Sophie.

And, before anyone could disagree, the girls turned around and whisked the tea things – including the elephant teapot and its rider – out of the room to safety.

After the guests had gone home, the sisters went up to their bedroom to watch the enchanted teapot snoozing in Scampers' cage. Scampers sniffed at it and went back to cleaning his whiskers.

'That was close,' said Sophie.

'Yes, it was,' said Zinny, appearing beside her. 'We found out it was the pixies. Mrs Milkthistle says their spell should wear off in three or four days.'

'That long?' asked Sophie.

Right on cue, the teapot lifted its head and gave them a wink.

'Looks like it's going to be an interesting few days,' sighed Ellen.

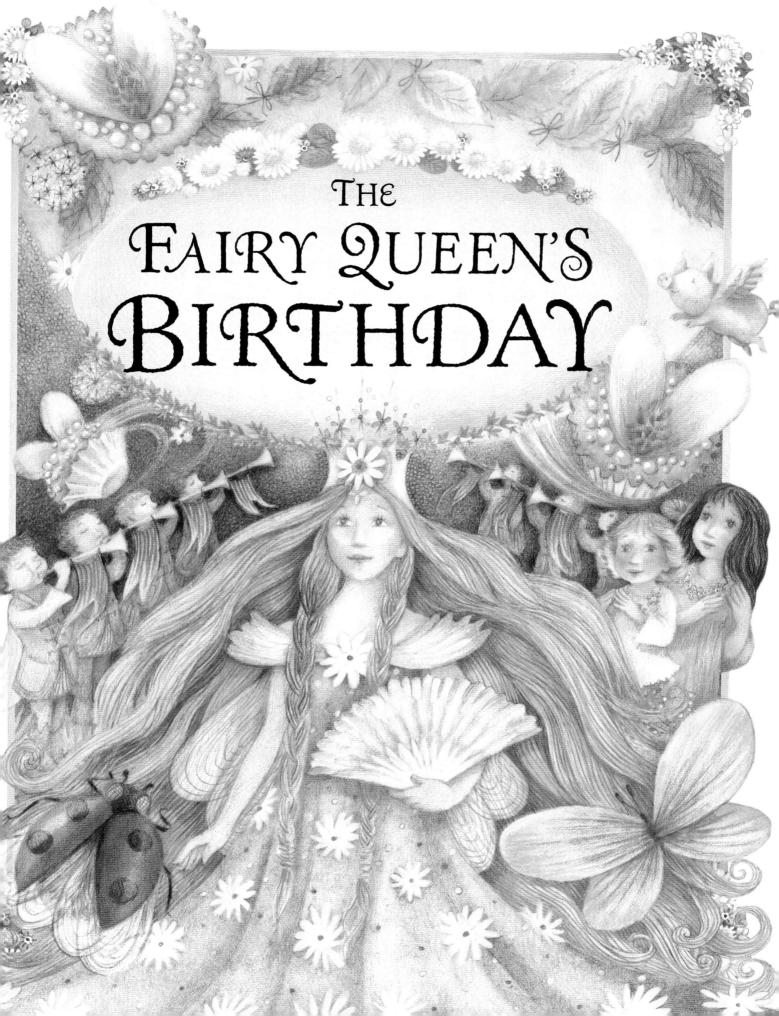

THE
FAIRY QUEEN'S
BIRTHDAY

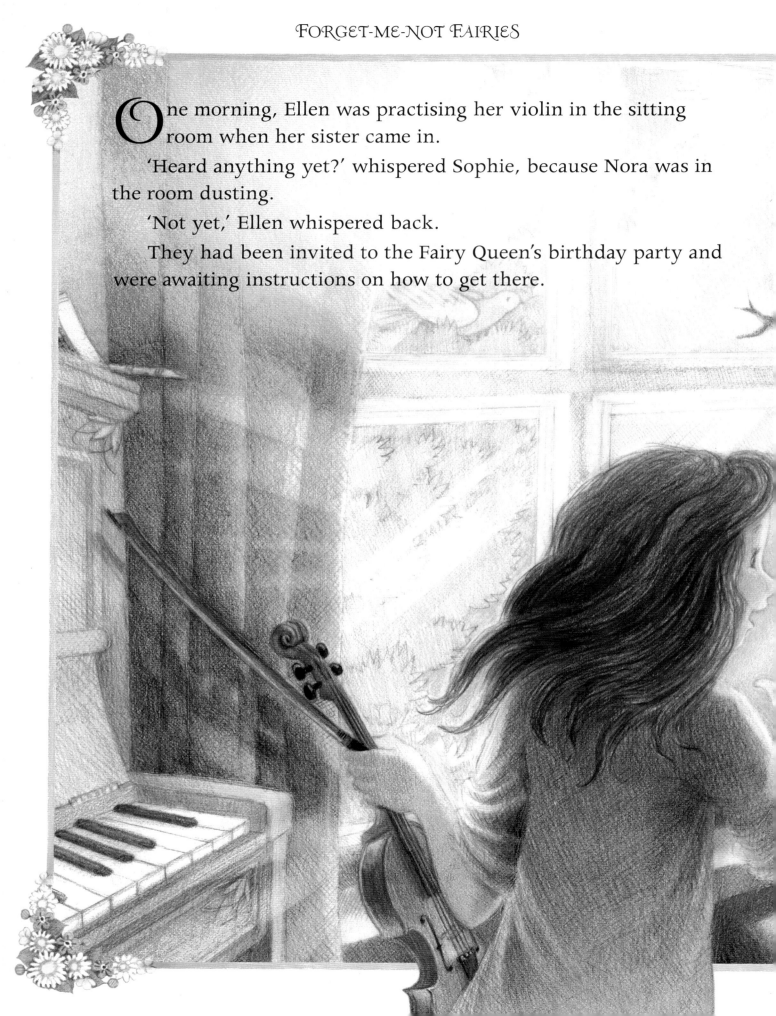

One morning, Ellen was practising her violin in the sitting room when her sister came in.

'Heard anything yet?' whispered Sophie, because Nora was in the room dusting.

'Not yet,' Ellen whispered back.

They had been invited to the Fairy Queen's birthday party and were awaiting instructions on how to get there.

'Goodness me, those pesky snails!' muttered Nora, pulling back the curtains. 'Just look what they've done to my windows!'

As the housekeeper bustled off to get a bucket of soapy water and a sponge, Sophie peered at the silvery snail trails. 'Ellen,' she said, grabbing her sister's hand, 'is that a map?'

Ellen looked more closely. 'You're right! It's a map of Wishaway Wood. X marks the spot where the party will be. Quick! Copy it down before Nora washes it off!'

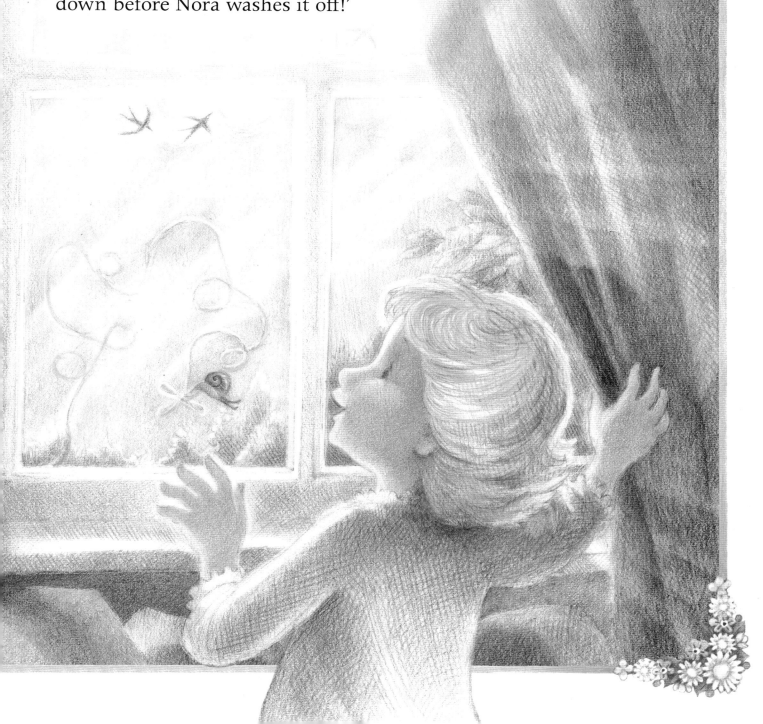

The moment breakfast was over, the girls slipped away to
Wishaway Wood. Following the map, they came to the village green.
The party was already in full swing. An egg-and-spoon race was
taking place with actual eggs and spoons racing each other. And
there was a group of fairies and pixies playing bowls using rolled-up
millipedes for balls.

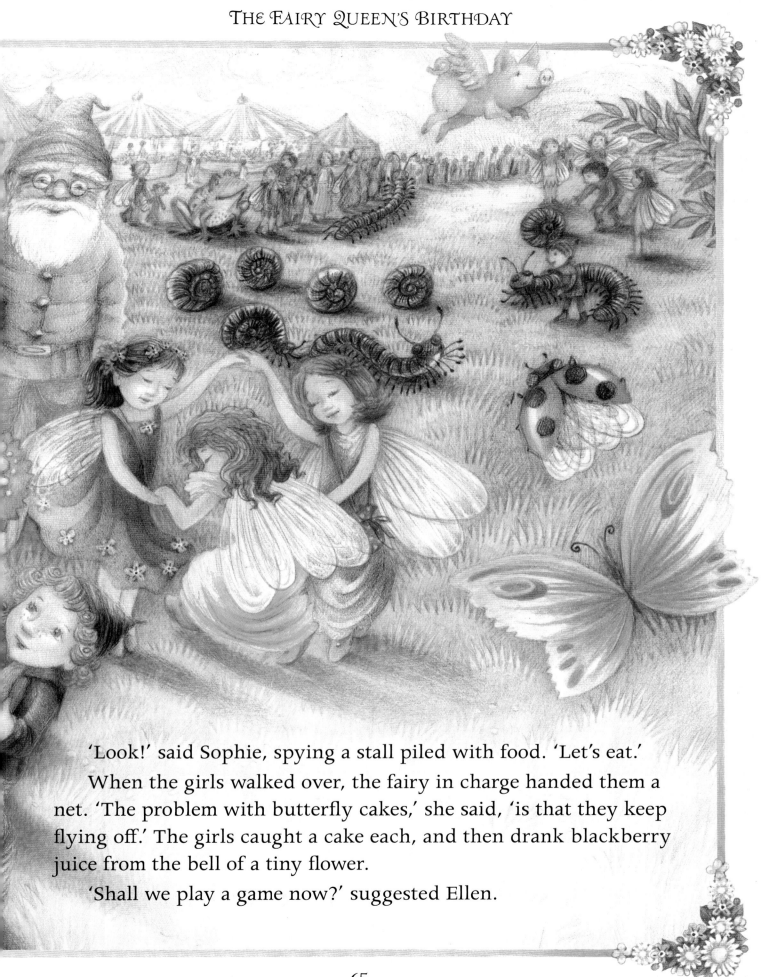

'Look!' said Sophie, spying a stall piled with food. 'Let's eat.'

When the girls walked over, the fairy in charge handed them a net. 'The problem with butterfly cakes,' she said, 'is that they keep flying off.' The girls caught a cake each, and then drank blackberry juice from the bell of a tiny flower.

'Shall we play a game now?' suggested Ellen.

Over by the hoopla, a rather cross Mr Nettles was shaking his fist at the prizes as they darted about on the table. 'Keep still!' he ordered. A pair of drumsticks flew up and played a drum roll on his head. 'Stop that at once!'

Sophie took a ring and aimed it at a prize on the table – a small flower in a pot. To her surprise, the flower caught the ring and threw it right back. Sophie caught it, and she and the flower played a game of catch. Mr Nettles's face grew redder and redder.

'There you are!' cried Zinny, running up to greet the girls. 'Come and join us in the three-legged race!'

Sophie paired up with Zinny, and Ellen paired up with Poppy. Then two caterpillars joined in, turning it into a one-hundred-legged race.

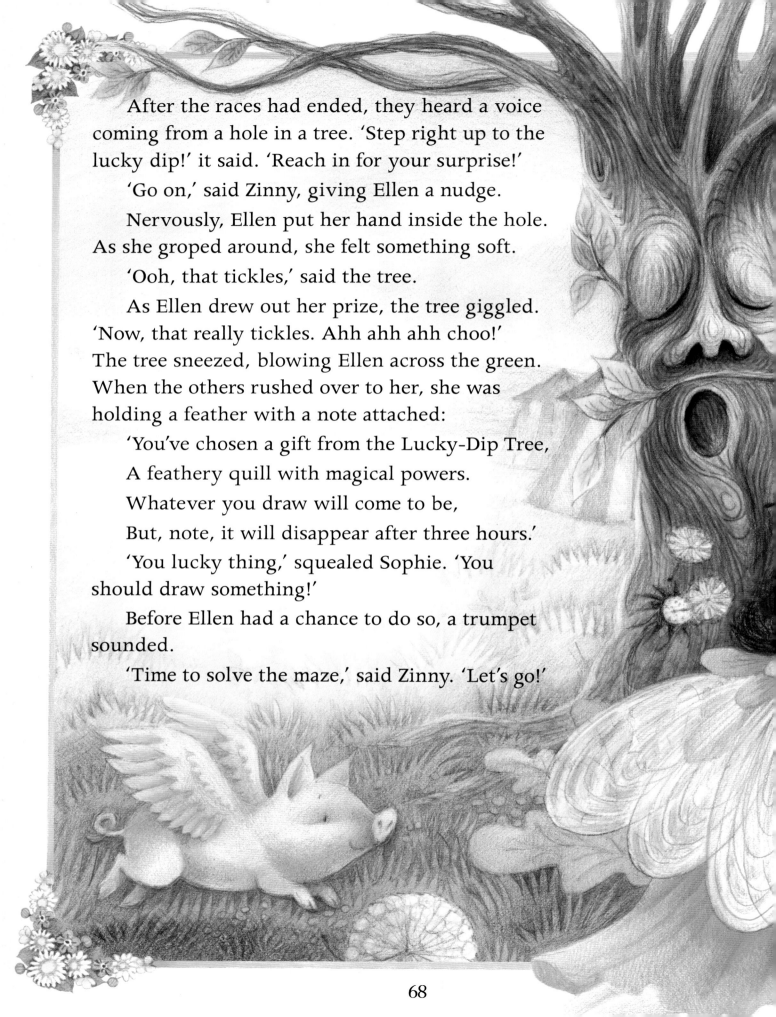

After the races had ended, they heard a voice coming from a hole in a tree. 'Step right up to the lucky dip!' it said. 'Reach in for your surprise!'

'Go on,' said Zinny, giving Ellen a nudge.

Nervously, Ellen put her hand inside the hole. As she groped around, she felt something soft.

'Ooh, that tickles,' said the tree.

As Ellen drew out her prize, the tree giggled. 'Now, that really tickles. Ahh ahh ahh choo!' The tree sneezed, blowing Ellen across the green. When the others rushed over to her, she was holding a feather with a note attached:

'You've chosen a gift from the Lucky-Dip Tree,
A feathery quill with magical powers.
Whatever you draw will come to be,
But, note, it will disappear after three hours.'

'You lucky thing,' squealed Sophie. 'You should draw something!'

Before Ellen had a chance to do so, a trumpet sounded.

'Time to solve the maze,' said Zinny. 'Let's go!'

Everyone gathered at the entrance to the maze – brownies, fairies, gnomes, clodhoppers (*and* pixies, although they kept out of sight).

A gnome cleared his throat:

'Come enter the maze two by two.

When you get to its heart, a surprise awaits you.'

'Clodhoppers first,' said Zinny, prodding the girls.

As soon as Sophie and Ellen stepped into the maze, the hedge closed behind them.

'Left or right?' asked Ellen, looking from side to side.

'Left!' said Sophie. 'No, right! No, left! Oh, I don't know! What do you think?'

'Right,' whispered a voice.

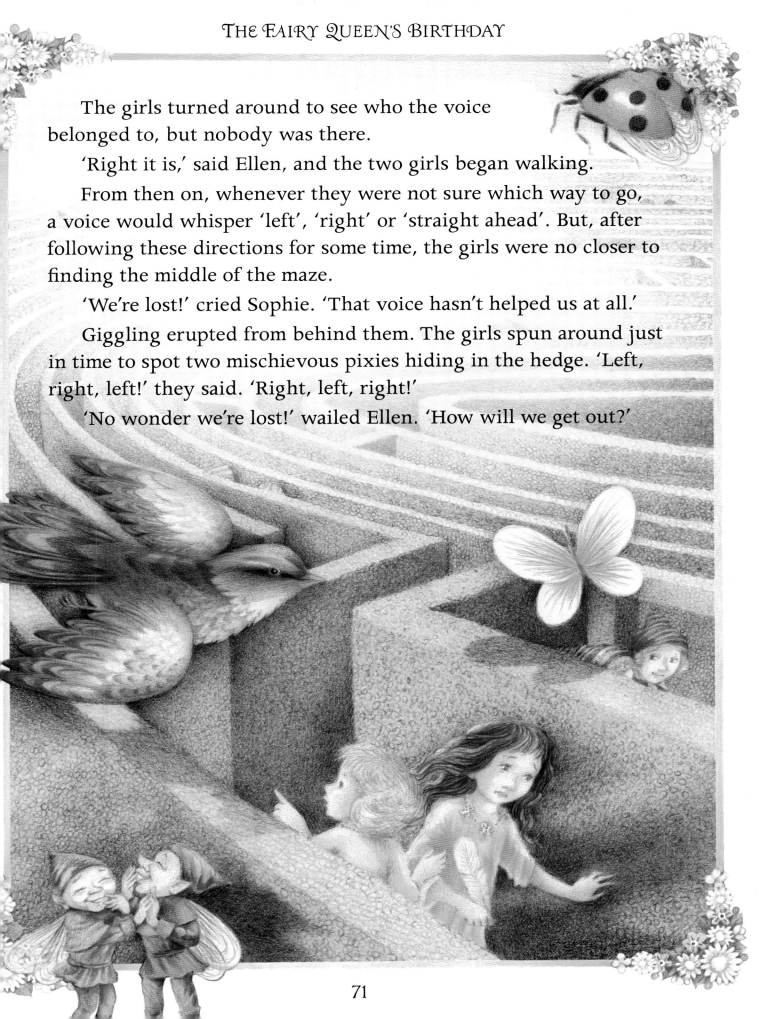

The girls turned around to see who the voice belonged to, but nobody was there.

'Right it is,' said Ellen, and the two girls began walking.

From then on, whenever they were not sure which way to go, a voice would whisper 'left', 'right' or 'straight ahead'. But, after following these directions for some time, the girls were no closer to finding the middle of the maze.

'We're lost!' cried Sophie. 'That voice hasn't helped us at all.'

Giggling erupted from behind them. The girls spun around just in time to spot two mischievous pixies hiding in the hedge. 'Left, right, left!' they said. 'Right, left, right!'

'No wonder we're lost!' wailed Ellen. 'How will we get out?'

At that moment, Zinny and her friends appeared above the girls. 'Where have you been?' asked Zinny. 'The queen is waiting.'

'We can't find our way out!' cried Ellen, close to tears. 'We're trapped in this maze!'

'Why don't you use your magic quill?' suggested Willow.

Ellen held up her quill. 'Of course! That's a fantastic idea! Thank you. But what should I draw?'

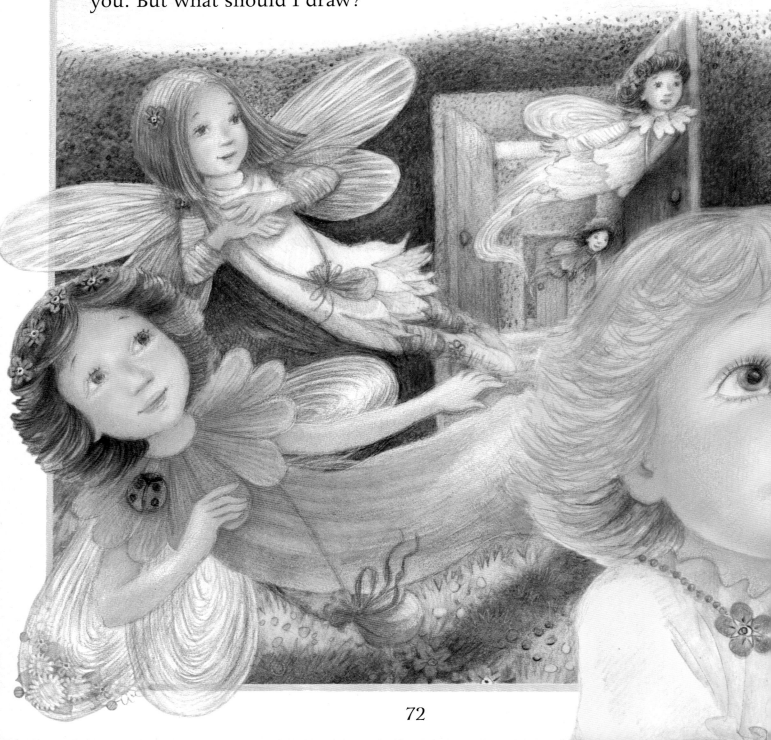

'What about a door?' said Sophie.

Ellen's eyes lit up, and she drew a door in the hedge. 'After you.'

Sophie opened the door and went through. Ellen followed. Then she drew another door, and another, and another.

'This is taking forever!' cried Ellen.

'Psst!' said Willow. 'Do you want a hint?'

Willow pointed to her green wings, and Ellen nodded. 'Turn around, little sis. This will get us there much faster.'

Ellen drew a pair of wings on Sophie, and then Sophie drew some on Ellen. They fluttered their wings and took off into the sky.

As the girls soared above the maze, Willow and her friends flew along beside them.

'This is brilliant!' declared Sophie, doing a somersault.

'I know!' said Ellen. 'And look! Down there!'

Directly below them was Queen Flora, surrounded by a group of fairies having a tea party.

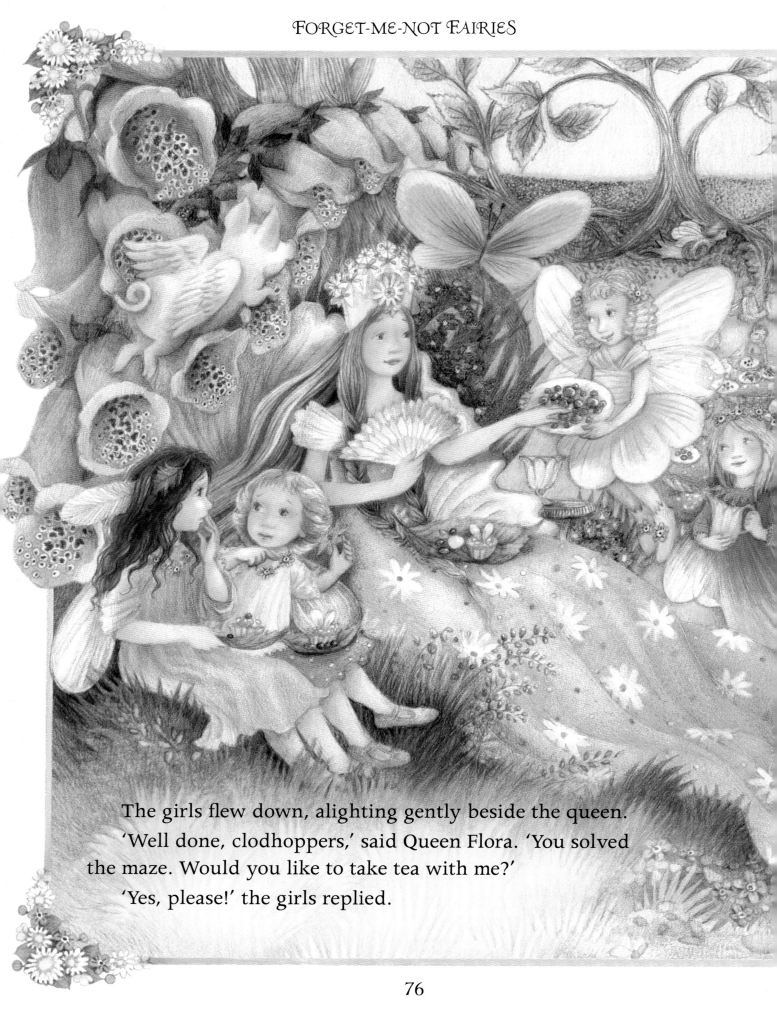

The girls flew down, alighting gently beside the queen.
'Well done, clodhoppers,' said Queen Flora. 'You solved
the maze. Would you like to take tea with me?'
'Yes, please!' the girls replied.

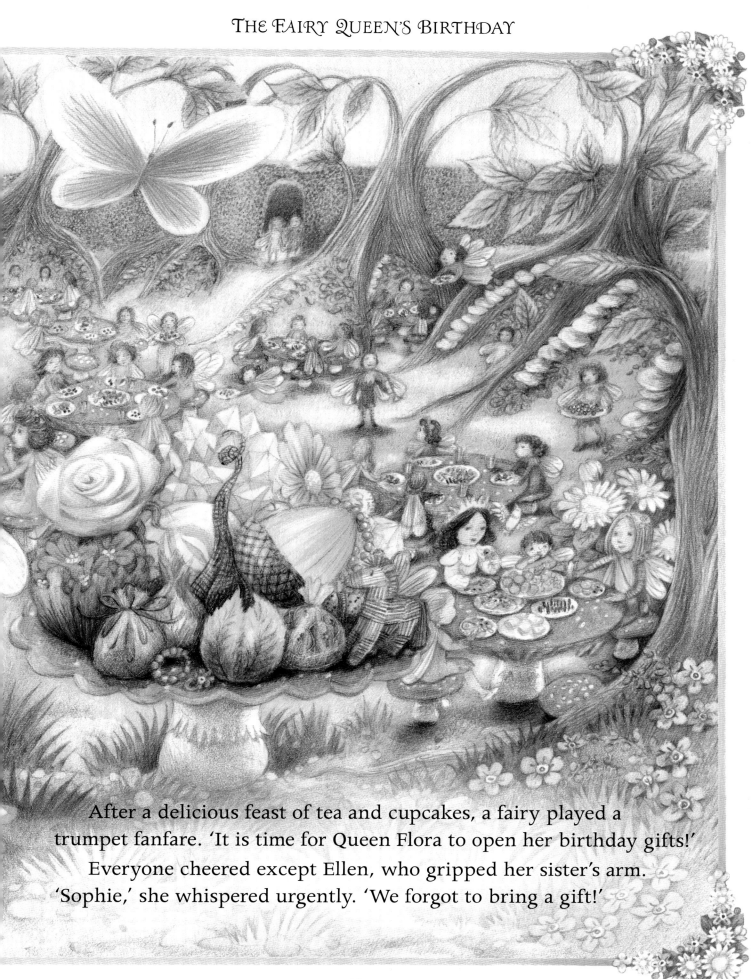

After a delicious feast of tea and cupcakes, a fairy played a trumpet fanfare. 'It is time for Queen Flora to open her birthday gifts!'

Everyone cheered except Ellen, who gripped her sister's arm. 'Sophie,' she whispered urgently. 'We forgot to bring a gift!'

Sophie thought for a moment, and then whispered something in Ellen's ear.

Ellen nodded. 'Queen Flora,' she said, 'for your birthday, Sophie and I would like to perform a special clodhopper's song.' With that, she took out her quill and drew a recorder for Sophie and a violin for herself, just like the ones they had at home. 'Ready, little sis?' And the girls played a jaunty tune while the queen rose to her feet and the fairies danced.

When the song came to an end, the queen raised her hand. 'I do believe this is the best birthday party I have ever been to.'

Sophie and Ellen could not have agreed more.

Butterfly Cupcakes

2 eggs
125g (4.4oz) butter, softened
1 cup caster (superfine) sugar
½ cup milk
2 cups self-raising flour, sifted
1 teaspoon vanilla extract

Topping
1 cup whipped cream
coloured sprinkles, to decorate

1 Pre-heat the oven to 160°C (320°F, gas mark 3). Place paper cases in a 12-hole cupcake tin.

2 Lightly beat the eggs in a mixing bowl, add the butter and sugar, and mix until light and fluffy.

3 Add the milk, flour and vanilla, and stir to combine. Beat with an electric mixer until light and fluffy.

4 Spoon mixture into the paper cases and bake for 18–20 minutes until risen and firm. Cool for 5 minutes, then place on a wire rack to cool completely before decorating.

Topping

1 Using a knife (ask an adult for help), cut a circle in the centre of each cupcake and scoop it out. Cut each circle in half, then set the pieces aside. These will be the wings.

2 Fill the middle of each cupcake with whipped cream.

3 Stand two cupcake 'wings' in the whipped cream of each cupcake. Top with sprinkles. You can also add marshmallows, a strawberry, a raspberry or your favourite topping.

Guide to Fairies

Wish fairies

Found:
* in the Land of the Clodhoppers collecting children's wishes
* singing and dancing around the Magic Ring of Toadstools
* listening to ladybirds whisper the secret wishes of clodhopper children
* polishing rainbows
* healing sick animals
* caring for the plants and creatures of Wishaway Wood.

Magical powers:
* invisibility
* granting children's wishes.

Likes:
* dancing
* singing
* playing leapfrog

Dislikes:
* broken promises
* mud fights
* fairy flu.

Fears:
* being seen by clodhoppers (with the exception of a few very special children).

Teacher fairies

* are a special kind of wish fairy
* wear a blue sash and a pouch to carry fairy dust
* carry a wand.

Found:
* at the Fairy School
* tending to the Magic Ring of Toadstools.

Magical powers:
* granting wishes to children
* casting spells with fairy dust or a wand.

Water fairies

Found:
* in or near water
* sleeping on mats made of woven reeds, floating along the river.

Magical powers:
* travelling by water, often popping up in ponds, puddles, icicles, streams and vases
* talking to frogs, turtles and fish.

Likes:
* playing tunes on icicles by tapping them with a twig

Dislikes:
* goblins' singing.

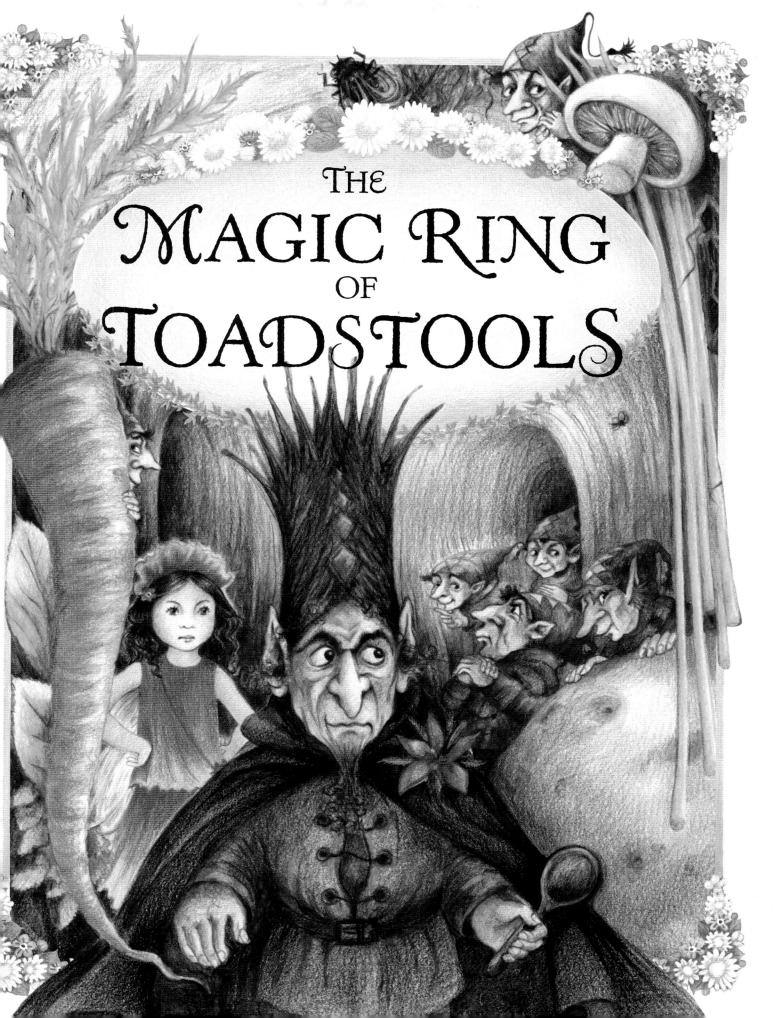

THE
MAGIC RING
OF
TOADSTOOLS

'I'm so excited!' said Sophie, clapping her hands.

'Me too!' said Ellen.

Zinny and Poppy had invited the girls to Fairy School. First stop was the nursery. Miss Lovage was rushing from cradle to cradle, tucking in the babies.

'They have a habit of floating out of their beds when they're asleep,' she said. 'When Zinny was born, I had to tie a piece of string to her toe!'

'Miss Lovage!' said Ellen, pointing at a baby escaping from her blanket.

'Oops!' replied the fairy. 'There goes Daisy!' And she flew over to tuck her in.

Next, they went to visit the toddler fairies who were learning how to fly. The toddlers took turns jumping off a small log and tumbling into the air.

'You're doing very well, my lovelies,' said Professor Bramble, catching a toddler in her arms. 'Flap faster when you take off.' She flapped her own wings to show them how. 'When Poppy was this age,' the Professor said to Sophie and Ellen, 'she was always doing tricks in flying class.'

'Like this?' asked Poppy, doing a triple somersault in the air.

Professor Bramble laughed. 'Like that. Now, away with you. Your class is about to start, isn't it?'

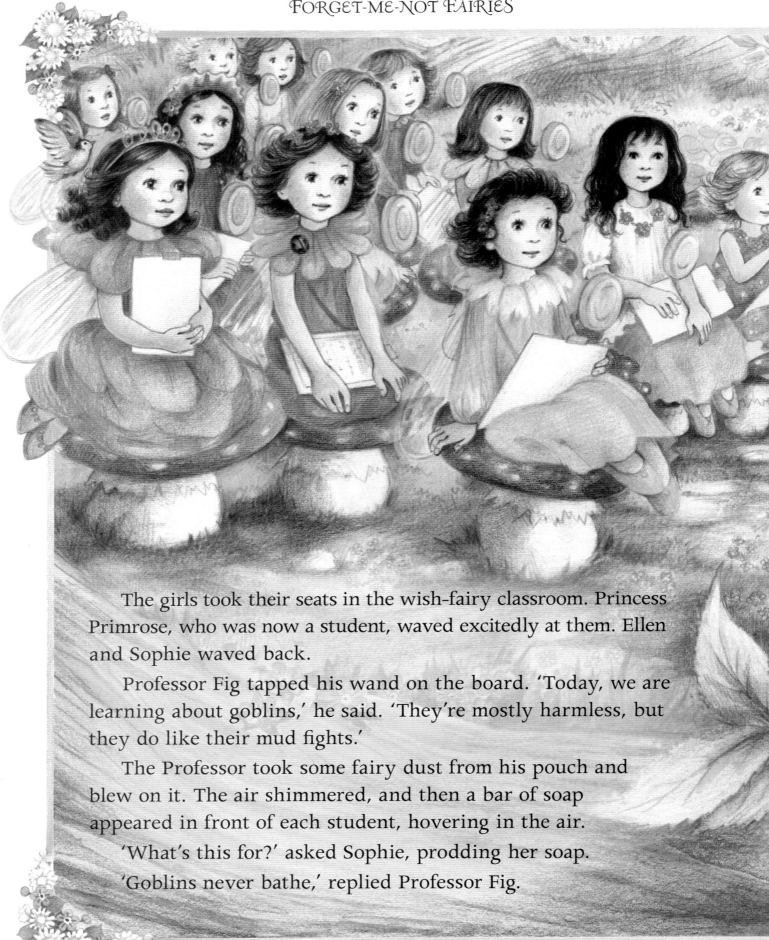

The girls took their seats in the wish-fairy classroom. Princess Primrose, who was now a student, waved excitedly at them. Ellen and Sophie waved back.

Professor Fig tapped his wand on the board. 'Today, we are learning about goblins,' he said. 'They're mostly harmless, but they do like their mud fights.'

The Professor took some fairy dust from his pouch and blew on it. The air shimmered, and then a bar of soap appeared in front of each student, hovering in the air.

'What's this for?' asked Sophie, prodding her soap.

'Goblins never bathe,' replied Professor Fig.

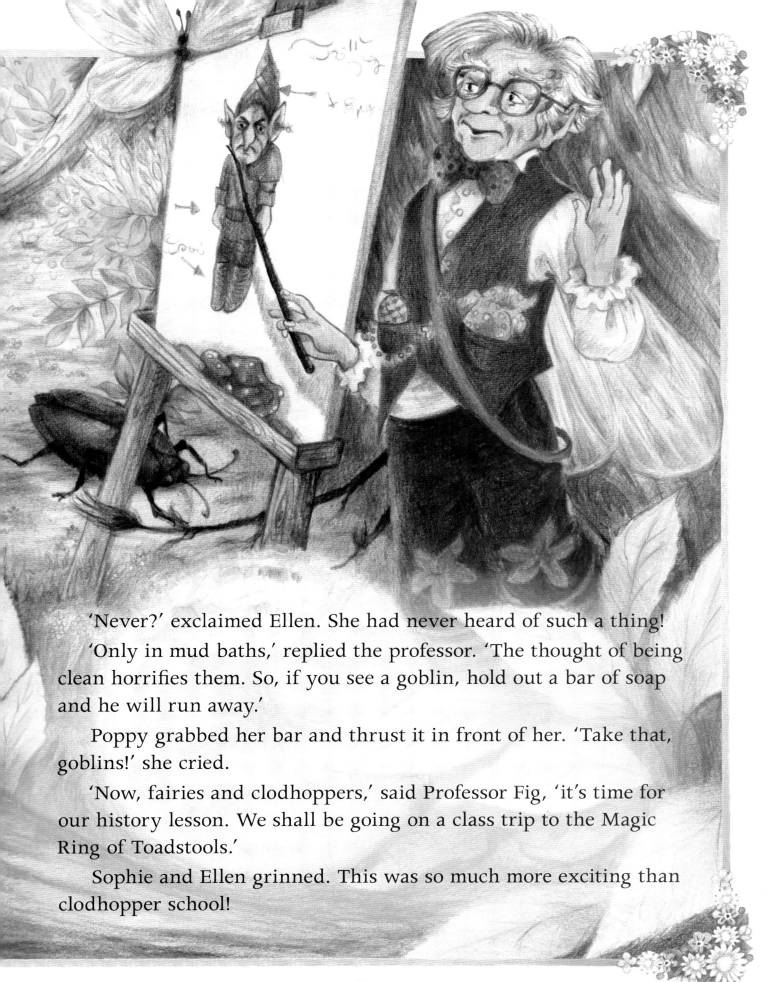

'Never?' exclaimed Ellen. She had never heard of such a thing!

'Only in mud baths,' replied the professor. 'The thought of being clean horrifies them. So, if you see a goblin, hold out a bar of soap and he will run away.'

Poppy grabbed her bar and thrust it in front of her. 'Take that, goblins!' she cried.

'Now, fairies and clodhoppers,' said Professor Fig, 'it's time for our history lesson. We shall be going on a class trip to the Magic Ring of Toadstools.'

Sophie and Ellen grinned. This was so much more exciting than clodhopper school!

Professor Fig led the way. 'Fairies have been dancing around the Magic Ring of Toadstools for centuries,' he explained. 'The ring is the heart of Wishaway Wood.'

But, when the class reached the clearing, the toadstools were gone!

'Not again!' cried Professor Fig. 'That's the third time this month!' He stalked about, examining the bare ground.

'Whoever keeps stealing them must be stopped!' cried Poppy, who could be as fiery as her orange-red dress.

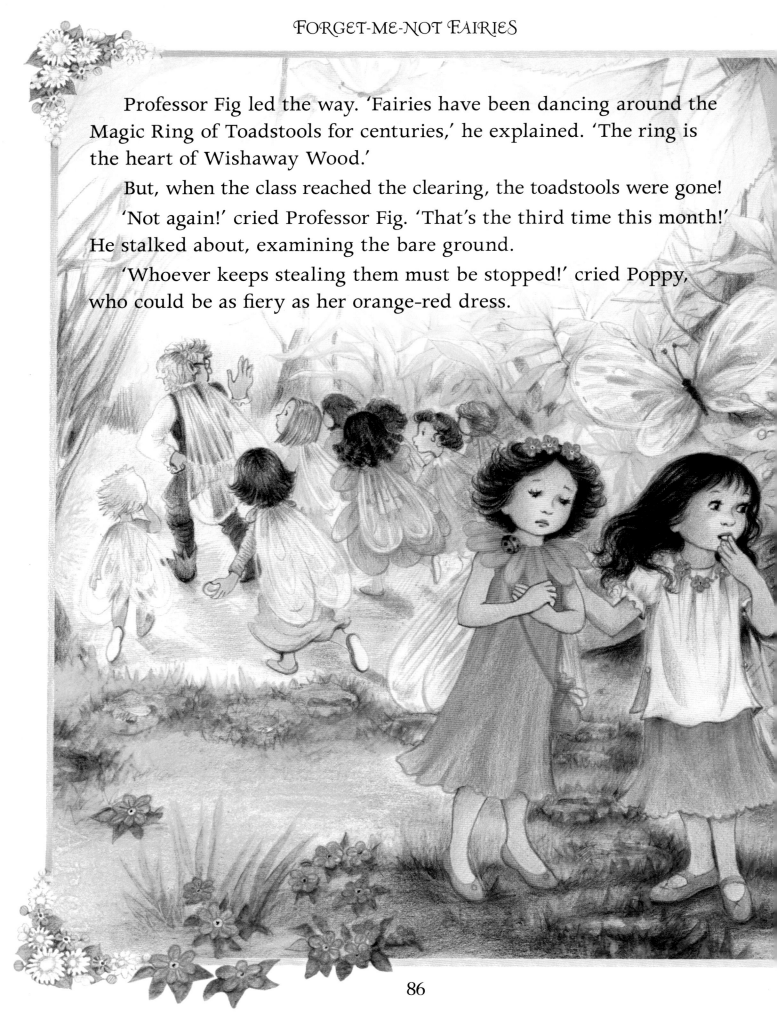

Zinny frowned. 'Without the Magic Ring of Toadstools, we can't grant any wishes,' she said to Sophie and Ellen.

'Back to class, everyone,' said Professor Fig with a sigh. 'The trip is cancelled.'

The fairies headed back down the path. Zinny, Poppy and the girls were about to follow them when Sophie gasped loudly. 'Look!' she cried, pointing to a trail of mud leading into the woods. 'Didn't Professor Fig say goblins like mud?'

'I think the answer to the missing toadstools is down that path,' said Poppy. 'Anyone feeling brave?'

The four friends travelled through the forest, boldly at first, then more slowly as the trees grew thicker.

'I'm scared,' said Sophie, holding Ellen's hand.

'It's okay,' said Zinny. 'Professor Fig said goblins are mostly harmless, remember?' Even so, she got out her bar of soap.

'Did you hear that?' asked Poppy.

Loud, out-of-tune singing was coming from over the hill. The girls and fairies crept forwards. There, before them, was a group of goblins having a party under a large dead tree beside a muddy pool.

'The Goblins' Grotto,' breathed Zinny.

To get a better look, the little group quietly crossed the muddy pool on the backs of some frogs. Then, they stepped onto the bank and hid behind some reeds. There, they saw Borage, the Goblin King, eating soup – toadstool soup!

Ellen's blood boiled, and before anyone could stop her, she stood up. 'You greedy goblin!' she cried. 'Stop that at once!'

King Borage looked up, and Ellen glared at him. 'You should be ashamed of yourself,' she scolded, 'stealing all those toadstools!'

The Goblin King stared back, looking very fierce. Then his bottom lip trembled. 'B-but toadstool soup is my favourite,' he whimpered. 'What shall I eat instead?'

Surprised at the Goblin King's tears, Ellen paused. An idea was forming in her mind. 'What if I make you some potato soup instead?'

All the goblins burst out laughing.

'*Eat* potatoes?' cried King Borage. 'How strange! We carve them into furniture.'

'Well, *we* think eating toadstools is strange,' said Sophie. 'They're poisonous to clodhoppers.'

'Besides,' added Ellen, 'potato soup is delicious. If I make you some, will you promise never to steal the fairies' toadstools ever again?'

King Borage tapped his chin. 'Only if I like the taste.'

As vegetables were so large in Wishaway Wood, Ellen needed the help of the goblins and the fairies to cut up the ingredients. One naughty goblin tried to throw a handful of mud into the pot, but Poppy held up her bar of soap and he scurried away.

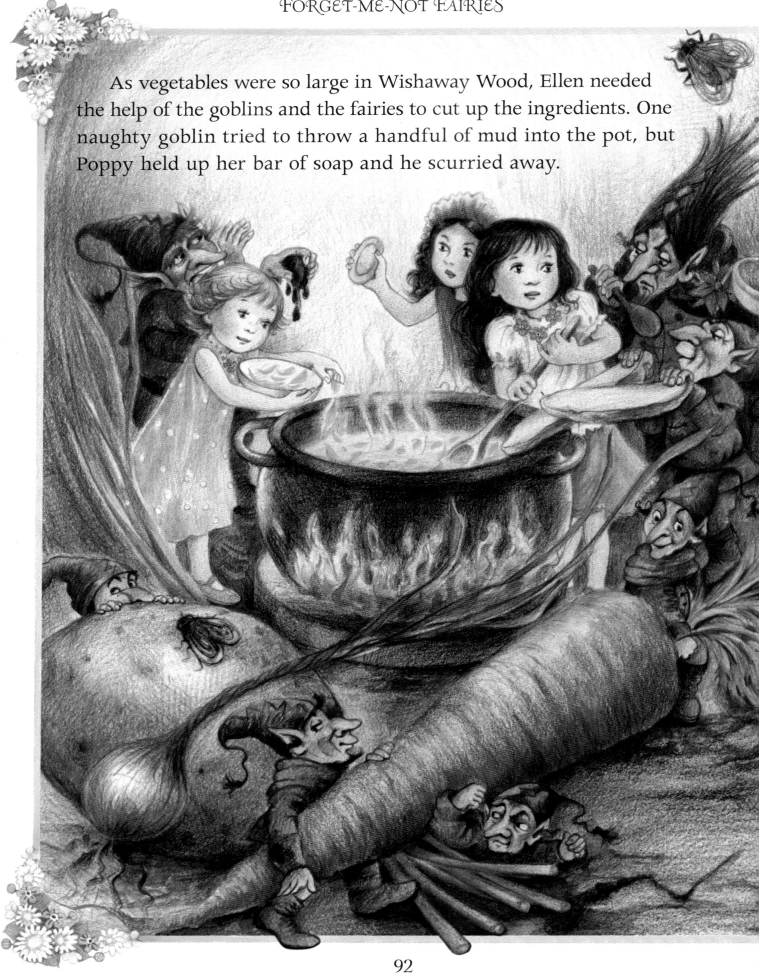

When the soup was ready, Ellen scooped some into a bowl and gave it to the king. He slurped a spoonful.

'Well?' asked Ellen.

King Borage slurped another spoonful, and then another. 'Mmm,' he said. 'This soup is delicious! You must give me the recipe!'

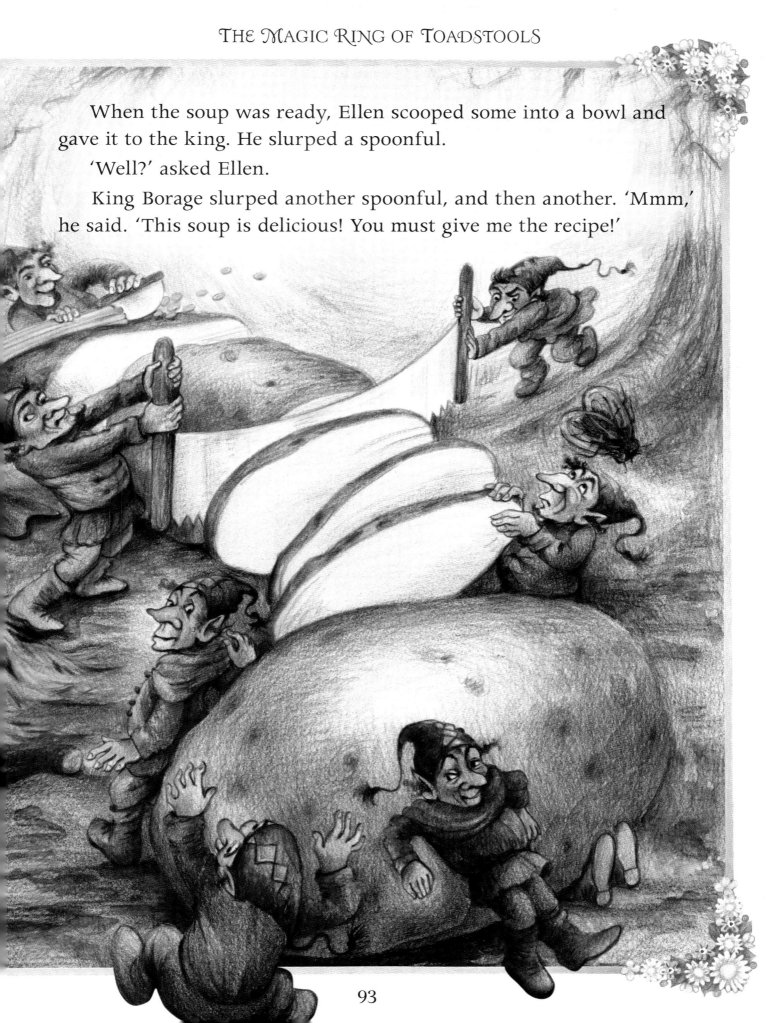

After Ellen gave the Goblin King her soup recipe, and the king promised to stop stealing toadstools, the girls and the fairies returned to the Fairy Village.

'Where have you been? I was so worried!' cried Professor Fig, too relieved to be cross.

Quickly, Zinny explained and they were rewarded by cheers and whoops from the crowd.

Later, the girls were invited to a special ceremony at the clearing. The piper played a tune, and the fairies skipped around in a circle.

As they sang, they tossed fairy dust into the air. The dust spiralled around and around, and then Sophie and Ellen heard what sounded like a heartbeat coming from deep within the Earth – *da dum da dum da dum* – the heart of Wishaway Wood. As the dust settled, toadstools shimmered into existence, regrowing before them.

Sophie's and Ellen's eyes sparkled, happy to know that because of their help (and a bowl of potato soup), the wishes of children all around the world would be granted tonight.

Guide to Magical Creatures

Goblins

* dimwitted
* long noses for sniffing out mud puddles
* large ears that swivel upwards to catch rainwater for drinking.

Found:
* in the Goblins' Grotto
* taking a mud bath
* in dark, smelly places such as a cave or an old tree.

Magical powers:
* making things disappear.

Dislikes:
* soap.

Gnomes

* wise
* guardians of all gateways.

Found:
* beside archways and gateways
* fishing.

Magical powers:
* can transform into a statue to disguise themselves

Likes:
* pottering in the garden.

Dislikes:
* being woken from a nap.

Brownies

* hardworking but shy
* some clodhoppers will leave a chair by the fire for a brownie to sit in and warm themselves.

Found:
* cleaning and mending in clodhopper homes
* sleeping under the floorboards.

Magical tools:
* a magical key that can open any lock
* an enchanted cloth that can clean anything.

Likes:
* shiny things.

Pixies

Found:
* in the Lost Forest Market selling clodhopper items to goblins
* in pixie hives.

Magical powers:
* superhuman strength
* can mimic the call of any animal.

Likes:
* practical jokes
* gold
* 'borrowing' clodhopper items.

Dislikes:
* mirrors.

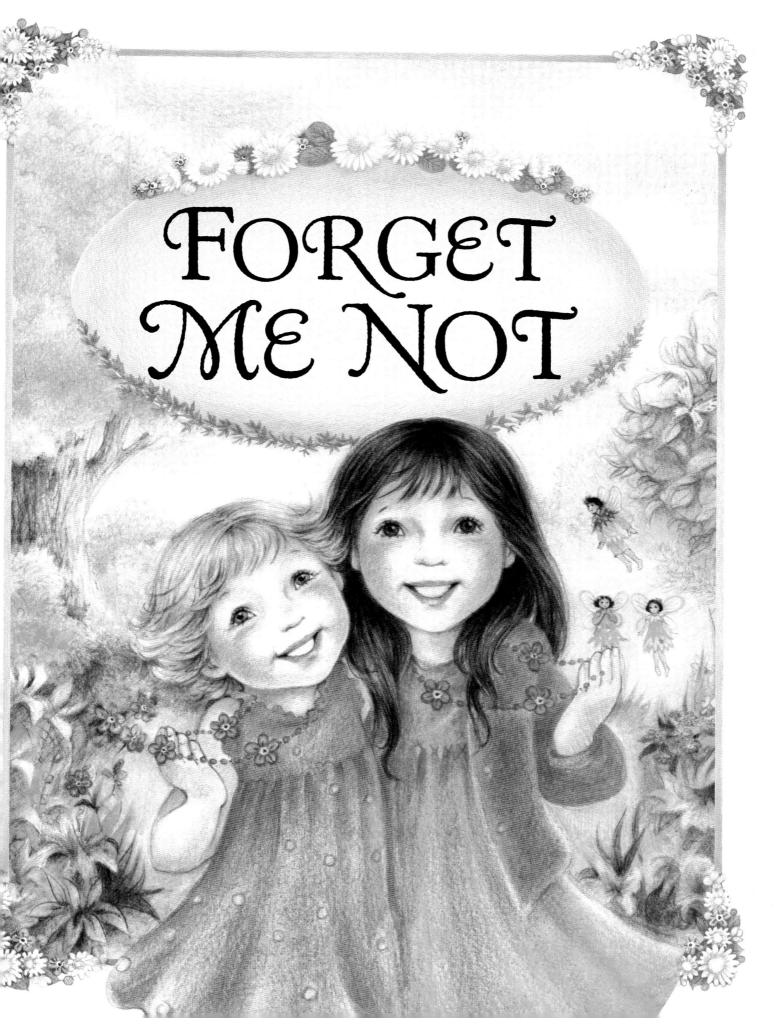

FORGET ME NOT

'All packed,' said Nora, patting a basket filled with delicious goodies.

'Yum!' said Sophie, peeking inside.

Veronica and Charles, the neighbours' twin niece and nephew, were visiting for the holidays. The grown-ups had arranged for Nora to take the four children down to the river for a picnic and a swim.

'I wonder what Veronica and Charles are like,' said Sophie. She and Ellen had never met them before.

Ellen waited until Nora went into the pantry, then she whispered in Sophie's ear: 'Remember, we mustn't breathe a word to them about Wishaway Wood.'

'I *know*,' replied Sophie, offended. 'I'm *good* at keeping secrets.'

When the twins arrived, Ellen and Sophie took them down the path to the river while Nora brought up the rear.

'Do you have any horses?' asked the elder twin, Veronica.

'No,' Ellen replied.

'*We* do,' said Veronica. 'I'm a very good rider, aren't I, Charles?' Before her brother could answer, she asked, 'Do you ski?'

'No,' replied Ellen. 'We like to –'

'We go skiing every year, right, Charles?' said Veronica. 'I'm a very good skier.'

Ellen pursed her lips.

'Here we are!' announced Sophie.

Nora laid out a rug by the river and unpacked the picnic basket. Sophie offered a crust to Scampers, who nibbled on it happily.

'I like your mouse,' said Charles. 'Is he –?'

Once again, Veronica interrupted. 'So what *do* you do for fun?'

Sophie and Ellen touched their forget-me-not chains and shared a look. 'We like to swim in the river,' replied Ellen.

'River?' sniffed Veronica. 'I'd call it a stream. I could swim across *that* in a moment.'

Ellen ground her teeth. 'It's harder to swim than you think,' she said.

'Oh, really?' said Veronica. 'Then how about a race?'

'You're on!' replied Ellen.

As the two girls changed into their costumes, Veronica said, 'Better take off that pretty chain, Ellen, or it'll be spoiled.'

As Ellen touched her chain doubtfully, Pip suddenly appeared at Sophie's shoulder. 'If she takes it off, she'll forget all about Wishaway Wood!' he whispered. 'Stop her!'

Sophie grabbed Ellen. 'Don't race!' she said. 'You know why.'

'Scared of losing?' said Veronica.

Ellen gritted her teeth and turned to Sophie. 'I'll be fine,' she whispered. 'You just make sure I put the chain back on after the race.'

'But, Ellen –'

She was too late. Ellen took it off and handed it to Sophie.

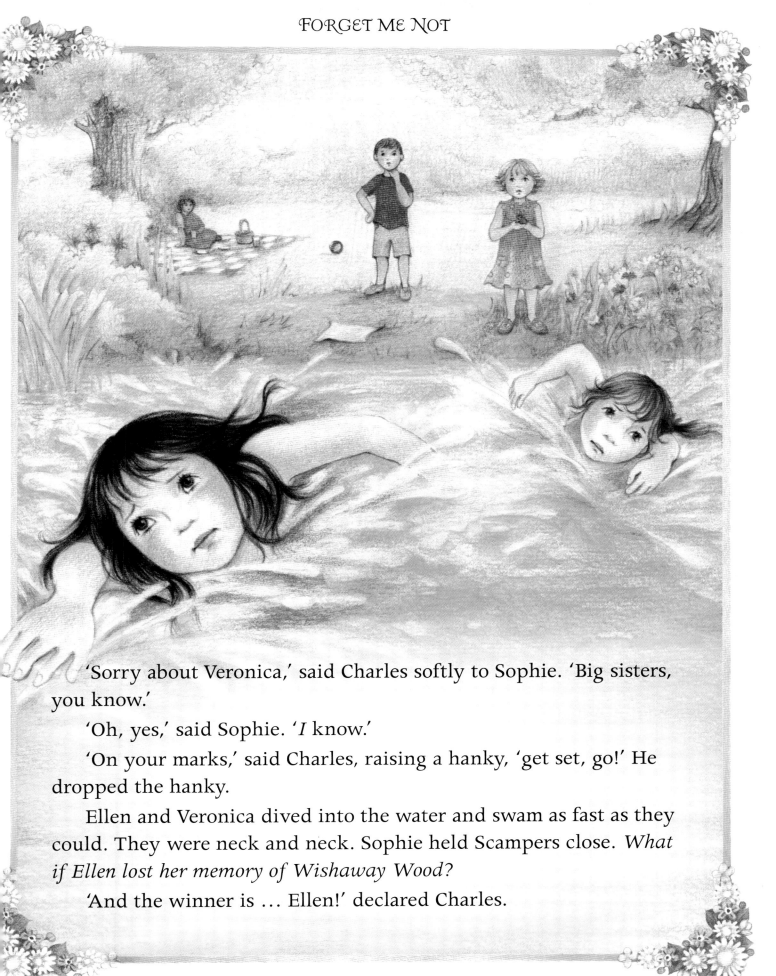

'Sorry about Veronica,' said Charles softly to Sophie. 'Big sisters, you know.'

'Oh, yes,' said Sophie. '*I* know.'

'On your marks,' said Charles, raising a hanky, 'get set, go!' He dropped the hanky.

Ellen and Veronica dived into the water and swam as fast as they could. They were neck and neck. Sophie held Scampers close. *What if Ellen lost her memory of Wishaway Wood?*

'And the winner is … Ellen!' declared Charles.

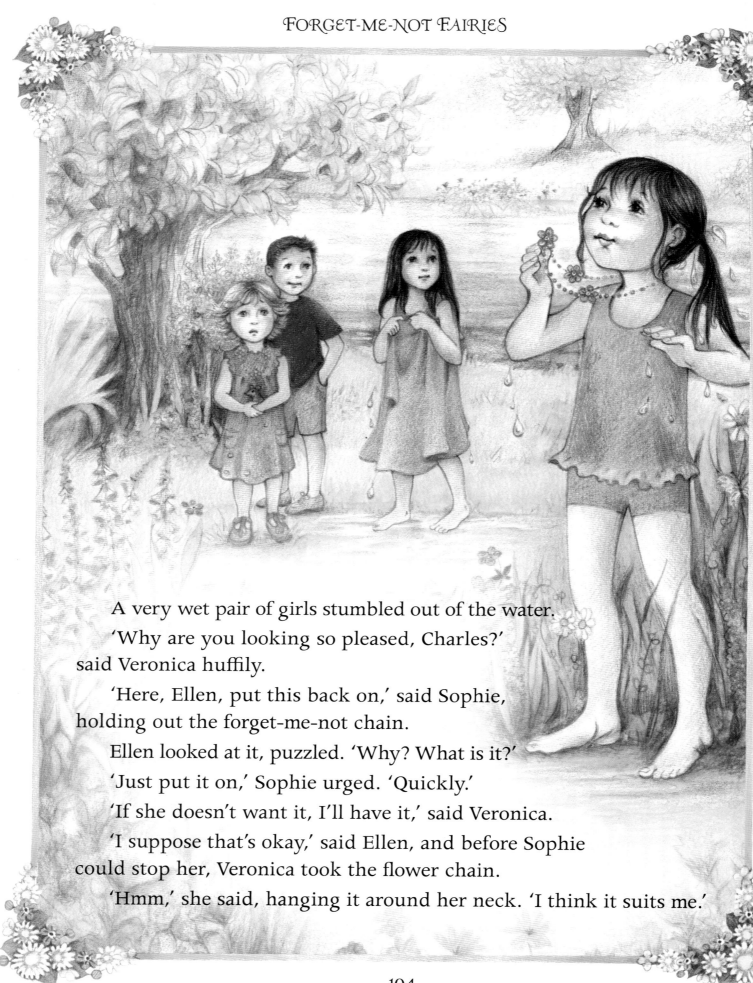

A very wet pair of girls stumbled out of the water.

'Why are you looking so pleased, Charles?' said Veronica huffily.

'Here, Ellen, put this back on,' said Sophie, holding out the forget-me-not chain.

Ellen looked at it, puzzled. 'Why? What is it?'

'Just put it on,' Sophie urged. 'Quickly.'

'If she doesn't want it, I'll have it,' said Veronica.

'I suppose that's okay,' said Ellen, and before Sophie could stop her, Veronica took the flower chain.

'Hmm,' she said, hanging it around her neck. 'I think it suits me.'

While Ellen and Charles finished eating, Sophie went and found Pip hidden in the reeds. 'There you are!' she whispered. 'Veronica won't get Ellen's memories of Wishaway Wood, will she?'

'No,' said Pip, 'but if the chain isn't returned soon, your sister will never remember the fairies. You must hurry!' Then he disappeared, and Sophie went over to Veronica.

'Can I please have the chain back?' she asked.

Veronica looked at her reflection in the river and smiled. 'No, I don't think so.'

'I'll give you anything for it!' said Sophie. 'Anything!'

Veronica's eyes alighted on Scampers. 'How about him?'

All the way home, Sophie could not stop thinking about Veronica's offer to swap the chain for Scampers. Her tummy was twisted in knots. Veronica had given her until later that afternoon to decide.

As soon as Sophie and Ellen got home, Sophie went straight to the birdbath. She picked up a stick and stirred the pool three times anti-clockwise, as the fairies had taught her. Then, she said the magic words:

> '*Water sparkle, water bright,*
> *Blue by day and black by night,*
> *Stir the surface, close my eyes,*
> *I bid you, water fairy, rise!*'

Suddenly, Pip burst out of the birdbath, splashing Sophie. 'You called?'

Sophie quickly told him what had happened. 'I don't know what to do! Either I lose Scampers or Ellen loses her memories.'

'This is very serious,' said Pip, gravely. 'But I have an idea that just might work.'

Later that day, Sophie went to the back garden to meet Veronica. Her hands were trembling. What if Pip's plan didn't work and she lost Scampers forever? And what about Ellen's memories?

'There you are,' said Veronica. 'Ready to trade?'

'I suppose so,' said Sophie, glancing at the nearby birdbath. *Come on, Pip! Where are you?*

Veronica held out the forget-me-not chain. 'Well?' she said. 'I haven't got all day.'

Just when Sophie thought she could not stall any longer, she heard a splash. The fairies had arrived! Next, she heard the soft murmuring of a spell being cast, and then she saw a fine mist swirling around Veronica.

Sophie hid Scampers behind her back and took a pinecone from her pocket. She rolled it towards Veronica. When Veronica picked it up, Sophie held her breath and thought, *Please let the spell work*.

Veronica stared at the pinecone for a long time. Then she said, 'Why, hello, Mousey!' and began petting it. 'Here's Ellen's chain back, Sophie,' she said, tossing it onto the ground. Sophie ran over to fetch it, laughing with relief.

'Thank you,' whispered Sophie to the water fairies.

Pip winked at her, and then he and his friends dived back into the birdbath to return to Wishaway Wood.

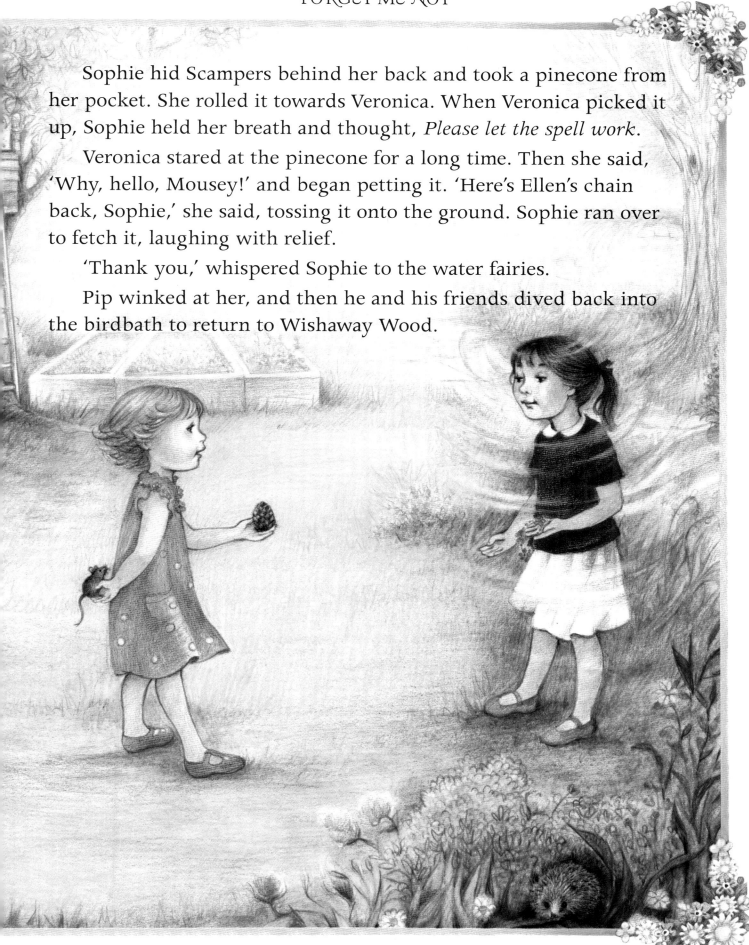

As soon as Veronica had gone home, Sophie went looking for Ellen. She found her taking a nap in the sitting room. Sophie lifted Ellen's head and placed the chain around her neck.

'Big sis,' she said, shaking her gently. 'Wake up.'

Ellen rubbed her eyes and yawned. 'How long have I been asleep?'

'A while. Listen, do you know who Pip is?'

'Pip?'

'Or Zinny? Or Bilberry?'

Ellen stared at her blankly and Sophie's heart sank. *Was she too late?* 'Please try, Ellen. Tell me how you get to Wishaway Wood.'

Ellen looked at her curiously. 'Through the archway at the bottom of the garden, of course. What a silly question.'

'Oh, Ellen!' cried Sophie, flinging her arms around her neck.
'Sophie!' said Ellen, baffled, but she hugged her sister back.

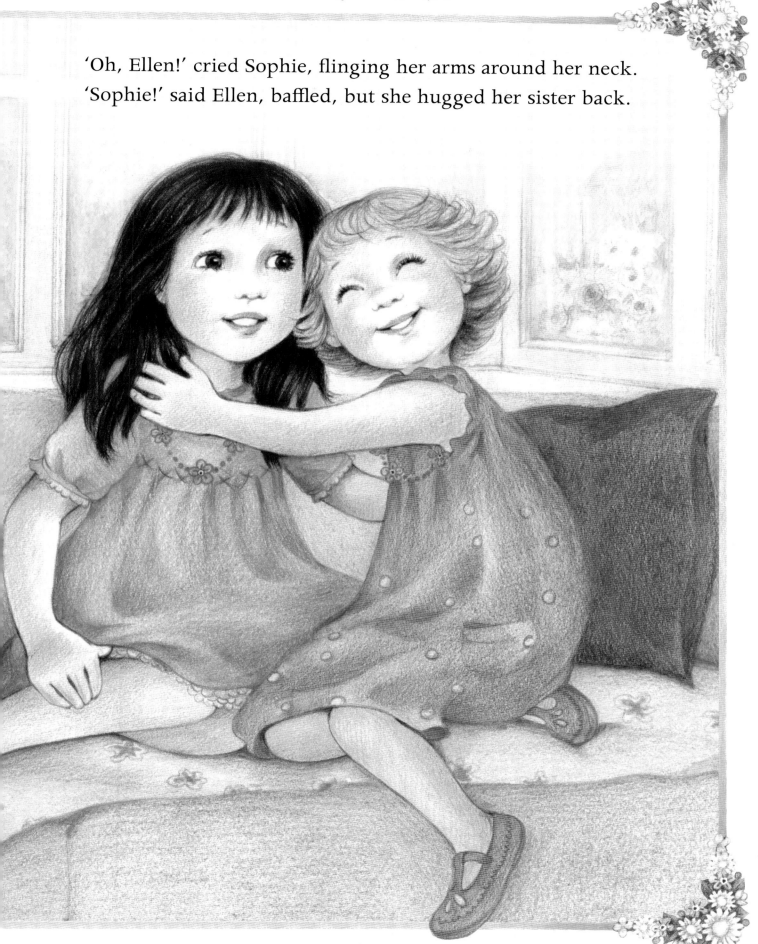

The next day, the girls invited the water fairies to a tea party in their treehouse. As they ate cake and biscuits, Ellen prodded Sophie in the arm. 'Look,' she said, pointing at the neighbours' back garden.

Over the fence, Veronica was walking around petting a pinecone while her brother was reading. 'Eat up,' said Veronica, giving the pinecone a piece of cheese. 'There's a good Mousey.'

Charles looked up from his book and gave his sister a strange look.

'What is she doing?' asked Ellen.

'It's a long story,' said Sophie, exchanging a secret smile with Pip. 'But I'm sure we've got some extra cheese if she needs any!'

Make a Flower Chain

You will need:
sheet of coloured paper,
scissors, pencil, 12 pieces
of dried macaroni,
80-cm piece of string.

3 When you have finished threading, tie the ends of the string together.

1 Cut paper into three flower shapes and poke a small hole in the centre of each with a sharp pencil.

4 To enchant your Flower Chain, lay it on grass and walk around it three times, saying the Flower Chain Enchantment.

2 Thread three pieces of macaroni onto the string, then a flower, then three pieces of macaroni, and so on.

5 Place your Flower Chain around your neck. You may now pass through the archway to Wishaway Wood!

Flower Chain Enchantment
Fairies of the garden,
Fairies of the stream,
To play with you each morning
Is my dearest dream.

Fairies of the sunshine,
Fairies of the rain,
Spread your fairy magic,
Enchant this Flower Chain.

WIDDERSHINS

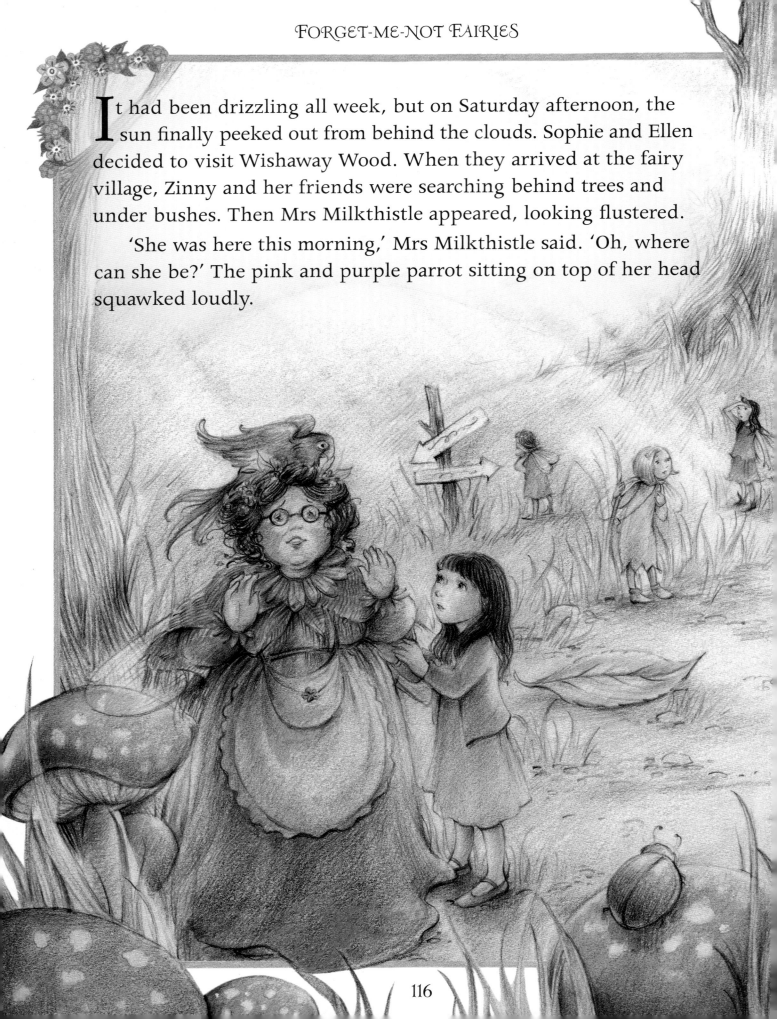

It had been drizzling all week, but on Saturday afternoon, the sun finally peeked out from behind the clouds. Sophie and Ellen decided to visit Wishaway Wood. When they arrived at the fairy village, Zinny and her friends were searching behind trees and under bushes. Then Mrs Milkthistle appeared, looking flustered.

'She was here this morning,' Mrs Milkthistle said. 'Oh, where can she be?' The pink and purple parrot sitting on top of her head squawked loudly.

'Who have you lost?' asked Sophie.

'Widdershins,' she replied, referring to her home. 'She's gone! Again!' Mrs Milkthistle's cottage had a mind of its own *and* a pair of legs. 'And just when I needed to get something out of the magic cupboard.'

'We'll help you find her,' offered Ellen, and the two girls looked about for clues.

'Look!' cried Sophie, pointing to a trail of very large footprints leading into the woods.

After the girls and the fairies had walked for some time, the trail of footprints ended abruptly.

'It doesn't make sense,' said Ellen, looking around.

That was the thing about Wishaway Wood. You were far more likely to find *non*sense than sense.

'There!' cried Sophie, pointing upwards.

Hanging upside-down from a tree branch was the cottage.

'Widdershins!' cried Mrs Milkthistle. 'Come down at once!'

The cottage swung itself upright, and then hopped playfully from branch to branch. Mrs Milkthistle frowned for a moment, but then a twinkle appeared in her eye.

'She's got that look,' said Zinny. 'Step back, girls.'

The older fairy tossed some autumn leaves into the air, blew fairy dust on them and whispered a magic spell. The leaves swirled, forming a red, orange and gold staircase.

'After you,' said Mrs Milkthistle.

Nervously, Ellen placed a foot on the leaf floating in front of her. Much to her surprise, it held her weight. She took Sophie's hand and, together, the sisters climbed the stairs to the top of the tree.

The fairies flew up to join the girls, but when they approached Widdershins, the door knocker blew a raspberry at them. Mrs Milkthistle muttered something about misbehaving cottages and turned to Ellen and Sophie. 'When I say "jump",' she whispered, 'jump!'

She gave the nod to Zinny, Poppy, Willow and Snowdrop, and before you could say 'pink and purple parrot', the fairies took a deep breath and disappeared. A moment later, they reappeared next to Widdershins and opened the door before the cottage could hop away.

'Jump!' cried Mrs Milkthistle. The girls and the fairies leapt inside the open door. For a moment, everything was still … then the cottage began to spin around and around.

'Oh dear,' said Mrs Milkthistle. 'Hold on, petals! I think Widdershins is taking us for a ride!'

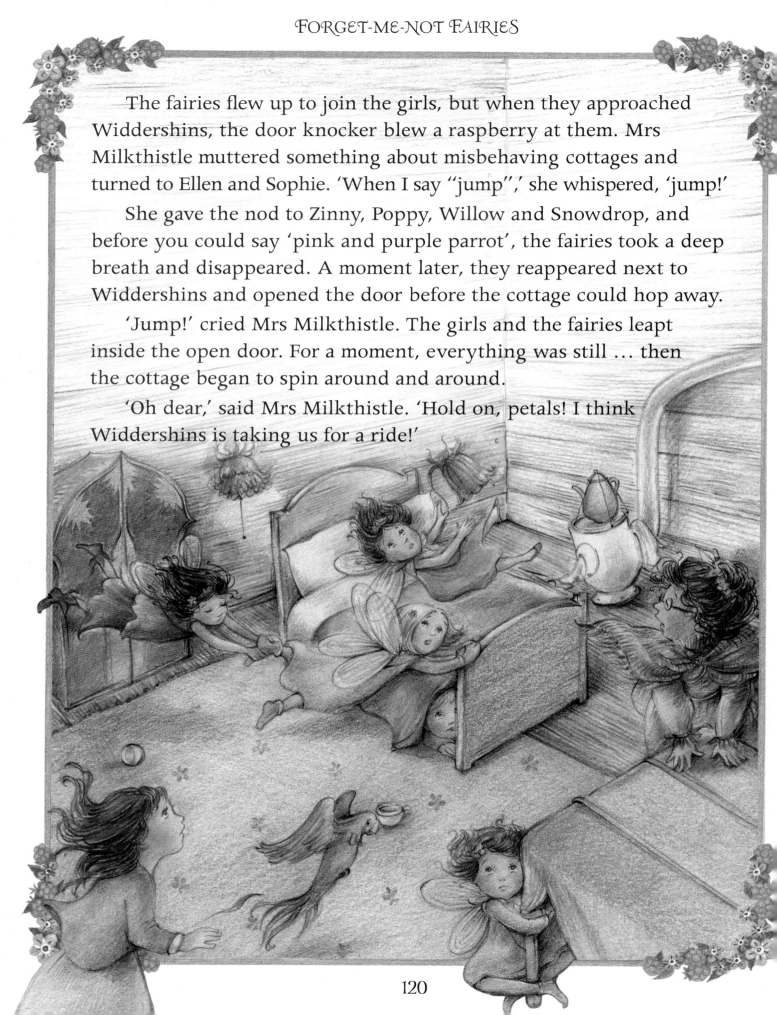

Faster and faster they spun. The parrot screeched in protest, while the girls and the fairies grabbed hold of the furniture to steady themselves. Up into the air Widdershins rose – up, up, up above the treetops and into the bright sunny sky.

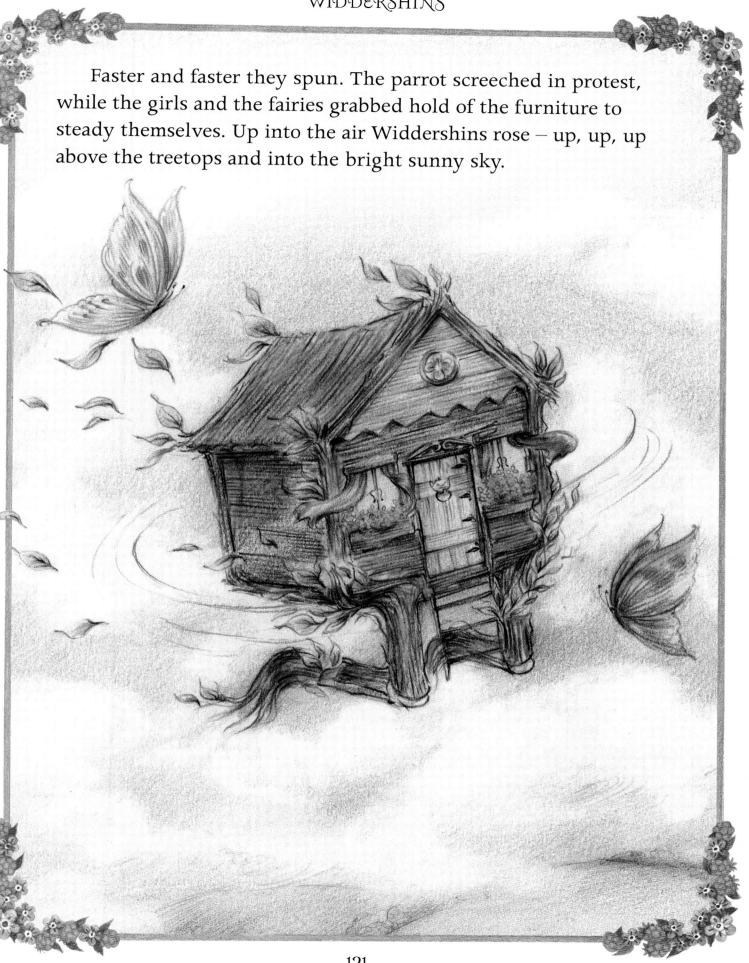

When at last the cottage stopped spinning, everyone ran to the window and peered out.

'We're up so high!' breathed Sophie.

Zinny clapped her hands. 'Can we look around?' she asked.

'Might as well, since we're here,' grumbled a slightly rumpled Mrs Milkthistle. She opened the door and stepped into thin air.

'Wait for me!' cried Sophie, and before Ellen could stop her, Sophie ran after the fairy.

'No!' cried Ellen. 'You'll fall!' She rushed forward to save her sister, but when she reached the door, Sophie was bouncing on a cloud.

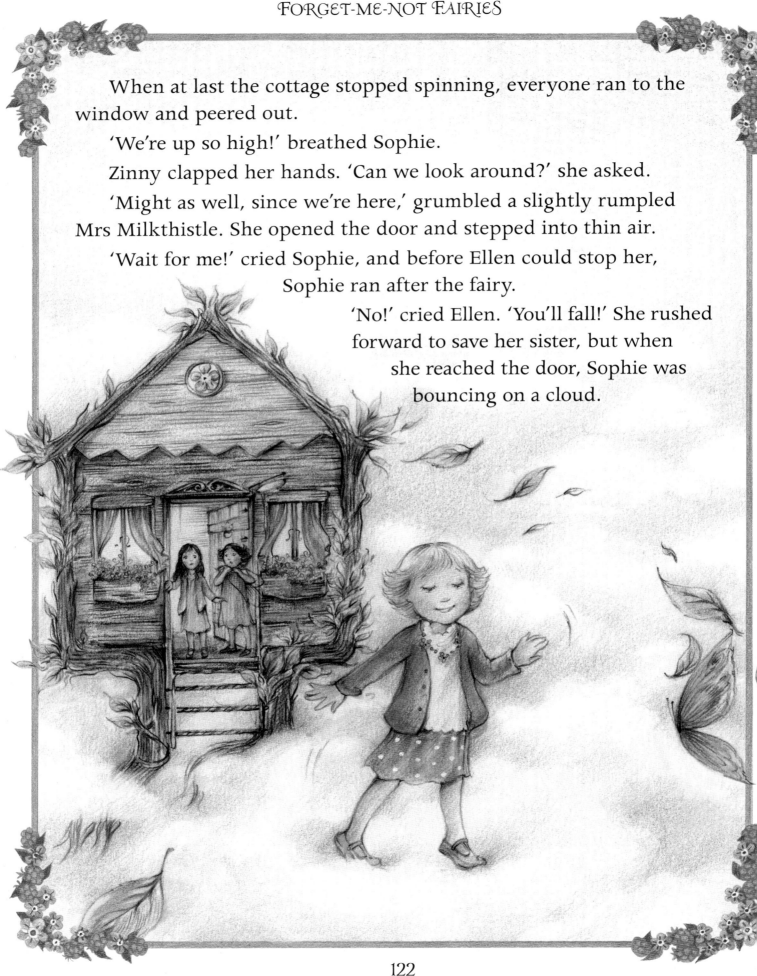

'Come and try it, Ellen! It's fun!'

Willow and Snowdrop led a doubtful Ellen outside.

'If you get hungry,' said Poppy, 'you can eat some of this.' She pulled off a chunk of cloud and popped it in her mouth. Each of the girls took a handful. The cloud melted on their tongues, sweet as sugar.

And so the fairies and girls spent a lovely afternoon, playing hide-and-seek among the clouds. When it was time to go home, Mrs Milkthistle clapped her hands. 'Widdershins!' The cottage peeked above a cloud, and then bounced away.

As they watched it disappear from sight, Ellen squeezed Sophie's hand. 'How will we ever get home?' she whispered.

Mrs Milkthistle smiled, untied a cord from around her waist and lassoed a nearby rainbow. 'Ready for the biggest slippery dip of your lives, my dears?'

Sophie grinned. Ellen gulped.

'All aboard!' cried Mrs Milkthistle.

The girls and the fairies hopped onto the rainbow and slid all the way back down to Wishaway Wood. 'Wheeeeeeee!' they cried before landing on a soft patch of heather.

'What about Widdershins?' asked Ellen, catching her breath.

'She'll come back when she's ready,' replied Mrs Milkthistle, glancing up at the sky. 'She always does.'

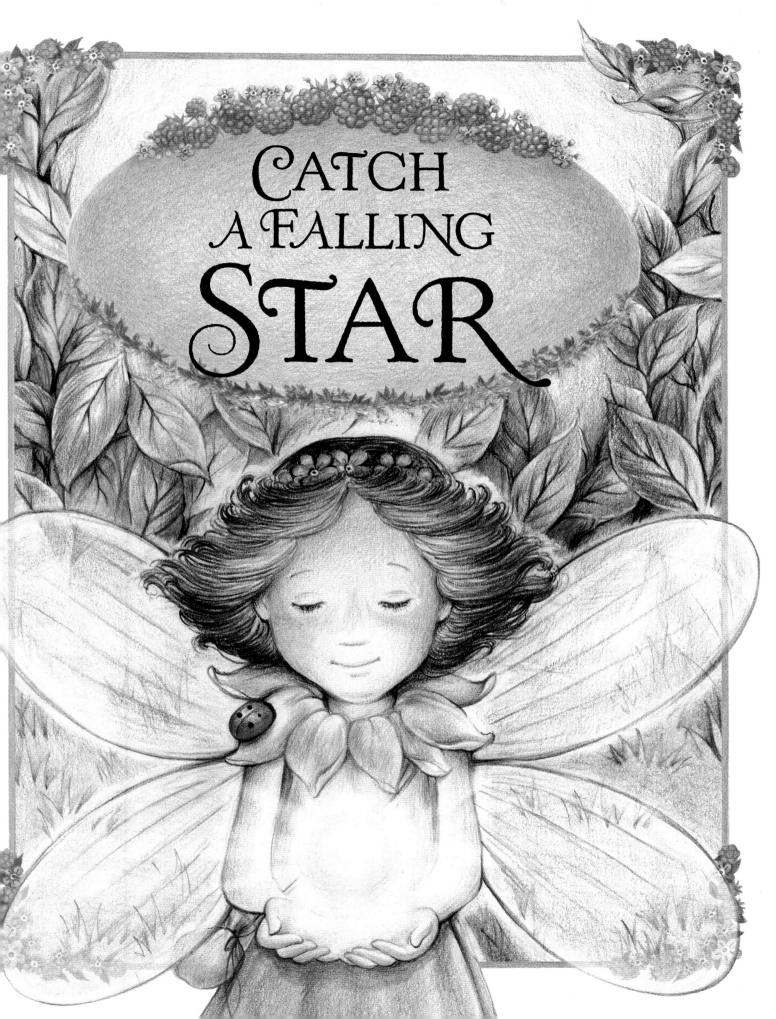

After a morning of chores, Sophie and Ellen decided to visit Wishaway Wood. There, they found the fairies playing a game of leapfrog.

'Can clodhoppers join in?' asked Sophie.

'Of course,' said Willow, fluttering her green wings.

'Zinny, are you coming?' asked Ellen.

The girls' best fairy friend shook her head, sighed heavily and plonked herself down on a toadstool.

'What's wrong?' Sophie asked. It was most unlike Zinny to pass up a game.

'It's Graduation Day tomorrow,' she replied. 'Apprentice wish fairies can't graduate from the junior class until they catch a falling star. I'm the only one in my class who hasn't caught one!'

'How awful!' said Ellen. 'Can't your friends help you tonight?'

'No fairy help is allowed,' Zinny replied, sadly.

Sophie and Ellen looked at each other. '*We're* not fairies.'

That night, the girls put on their jackets and slipped through the forget-me-not archway. They had arranged to meet Zinny on a hill at the edge of Wishaway Wood. As they lay back on a bed of leaves, the stars sparkled in the sky like a handful of diamonds scattered across a velvet cloak.

At first, the girls were hopeful that Zinny would catch a falling star. But, as the night wore on and none appeared, Zinny became downcast. 'It's no good! I'm never going to graduate.'

Ellen patted her hand. 'Don't give up yet.'

'That's right,' said Sophie. 'Look!'

A tiny star arced across the sky and tumbled towards Earth.

The trio trekked through the woods until at last they came to a clearing. There, lying on the grass, was the star quietly twinkling.

'Shh,' said Zinny. 'Fallen stars can be jumpy.'

Sophie went to the left and Ellen to the right while Zinny crept forwards, her net raised. She slapped it down. Too late! The star hopped away. Ellen reached out to grab it, but the star was too quick and skipped into the woods.

'That way!' cried Sophie.

Zinny flew through the woods with Sophie and Ellen running close behind. When they reached the fairy pond, they found the star hopping from lily pad to lily pad.

'Why not try the invisibility trick?' Ellen whispered to Zinny.

Zinny nodded, held her breath and disappeared. All they could see was a net suspended in midair, slowly moving across the water. The net came down, but not quickly enough. There was a tremendous splash followed by a very wet fairy emerging from the pond.

'That star's playing a joke on you,' said Sophie.

'Not a very funny one,' replied Zinny, wringing out her dress. 'But I'm not giving up!'

Without warning, Zinny lunged at the star and caught it, but the star did not lie still. It flew straight up into the air, taking Zinny with it. Ellen grabbed hold of the fairy's ankle to try to keep her grounded, and Sophie, in turn, grabbed Ellen. The star hauled them up, up, up into the velvety night as cool air rushed past their faces.

'Hold on tight!' cried Zinny as the star did loop-the-loops.

Then it hurtled back down to Wishaway Wood, skimming across the treetops. Sophie giggled as the leaves brushed her legs.

'How can you laugh at a time like this?' cried Ellen.

'I can't help it,' Sophie called back. 'It tickles.'

As the star towed them above the woods, Zinny's grip began to loosen. 'Can't - hold - on - much - longer,' she gasped, and with that, she let go.

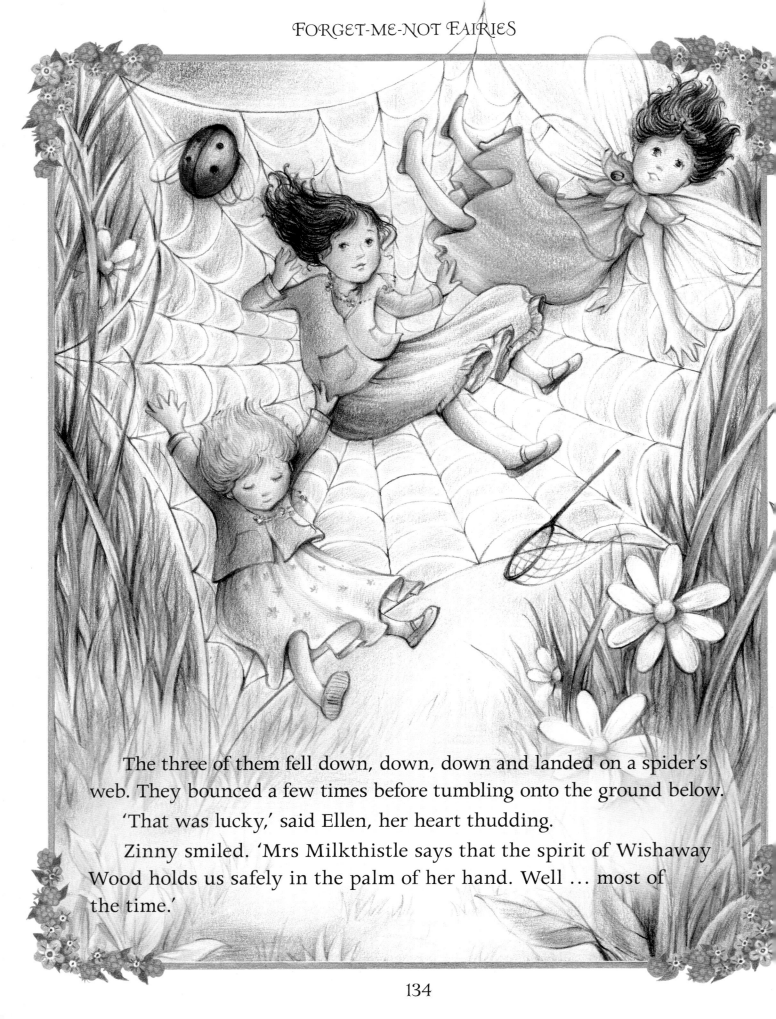

The three of them fell down, down, down and landed on a spider's web. They bounced a few times before tumbling onto the ground below.

'That was lucky,' said Ellen, her heart thudding.

Zinny smiled. 'Mrs Milkthistle says that the spirit of Wishaway Wood holds us safely in the palm of her hand. Well … most of the time.'

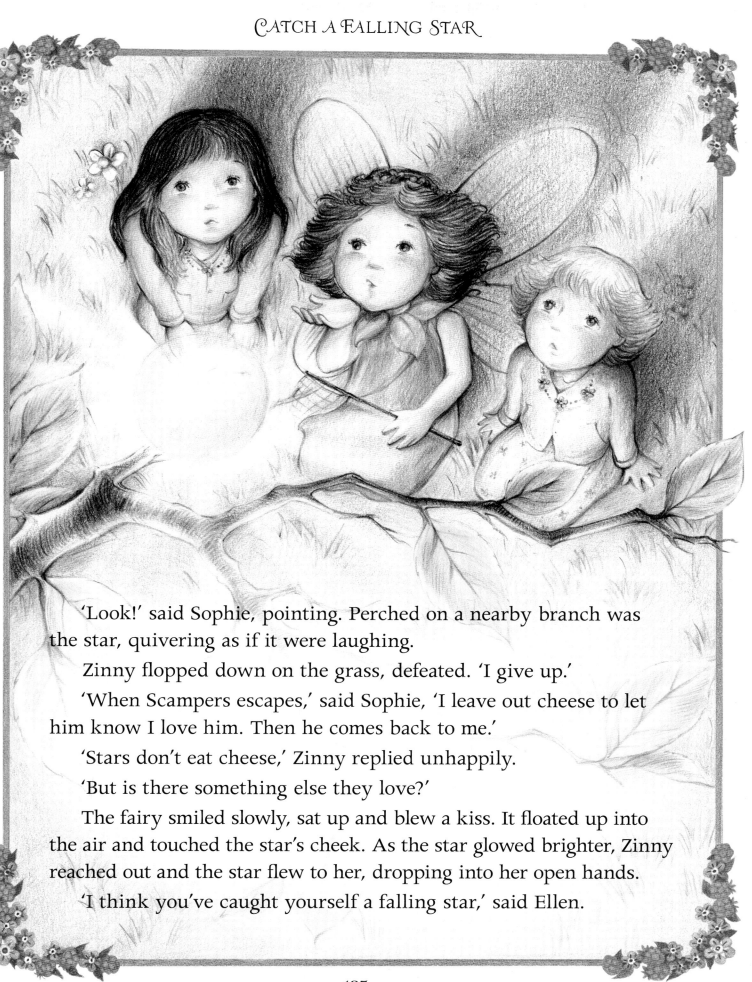

'Look!' said Sophie, pointing. Perched on a nearby branch was the star, quivering as if it were laughing.

Zinny flopped down on the grass, defeated. 'I give up.'

'When Scampers escapes,' said Sophie, 'I leave out cheese to let him know I love him. Then he comes back to me.'

'Stars don't eat cheese,' Zinny replied unhappily.

'But is there something else they love?'

The fairy smiled slowly, sat up and blew a kiss. It floated up into the air and touched the star's cheek. As the star glowed brighter, Zinny reached out and the star flew to her, dropping into her open hands.

'I think you've caught yourself a falling star,' said Ellen.

The next day, the girls put on their best dresses. They had been invited to attend the Wish Fairy Graduation Ceremony. Everyone was going – brownies, pixies, gnomes and, of course, the wish fairies. Zinny looked terribly pretty in her graduation dress.

'That's our Zinny,' said Bilberry proudly.

When it was time to begin, Poppy, Willow, Snowdrop and the rest of the class took turns being presented on stage.

'And last but not least,' said Professor Fig, beaming at the little pink fairy, 'please step forward, Zinnia Petal Blossom Birdsong.'

The crowd burst into applause, flapping and clapping. Zinny blushed and flew onto the stage to receive her wand. As she knelt before Professor Fig, he tapped her on the top of her head. 'For fulfilling the requirements of your forget-me-not training, I hereby name you a wish fairy proper. Congratulations on passing your junior training. You are now able to begin advanced classes in granting wishes.' He held out her wand. As Zinny took it, the star on the end glowed warmly. Zinny took a bow.

'Yes, yes, thank you, that will be all,' said Professor Fig as Zinny pirouetted across the stage. 'And now it's time for tea and cake!'

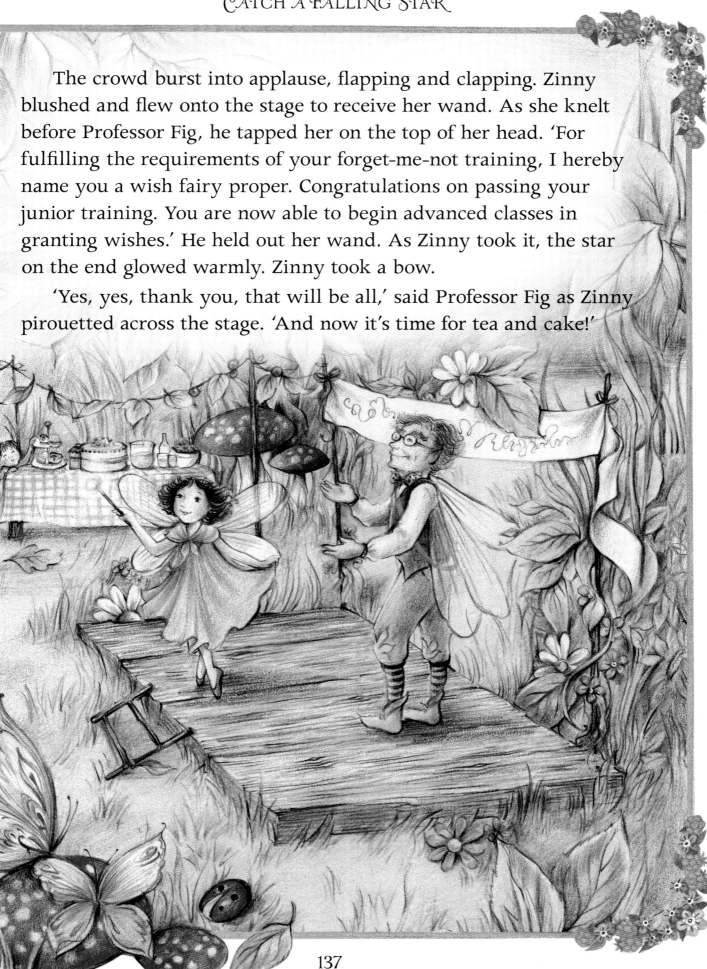

After a delicious supper, it was time for the girls to go home.

'Before you leave,' said Zinny, 'to thank you for your help last night, I'm going to cast my very first spell with my new wand just for you two.'

Sophie's and Ellen's eyes gleamed with excitement.

Sophie looked down at the empty bowl in her hands. 'Could we wish for a bowl of ice-cream that never runs out?' she asked.

'Done!' cried Zinny, and waved her magic wand.

The girls gasped with delight as Sophie's bowl filled with strawberry ice-cream. But before they could try some, the ice-cream kept growing, spilling over the sides to form a puddle at their feet.

'Uh oh,' said Zinny.

It didn't stop there. The ice-cream grew and grew, covering the ground. Without a moment to lose, Mrs Milkthistle conjured a raft. Bilberry jumped on board and lifted the girls to safety.

'Hm …' said Zinny, fluttering above them. 'I think my spells may need a little work.'

'Just a little,' said Sophie, and everyone burst out laughing.

Make a Fairy Wand

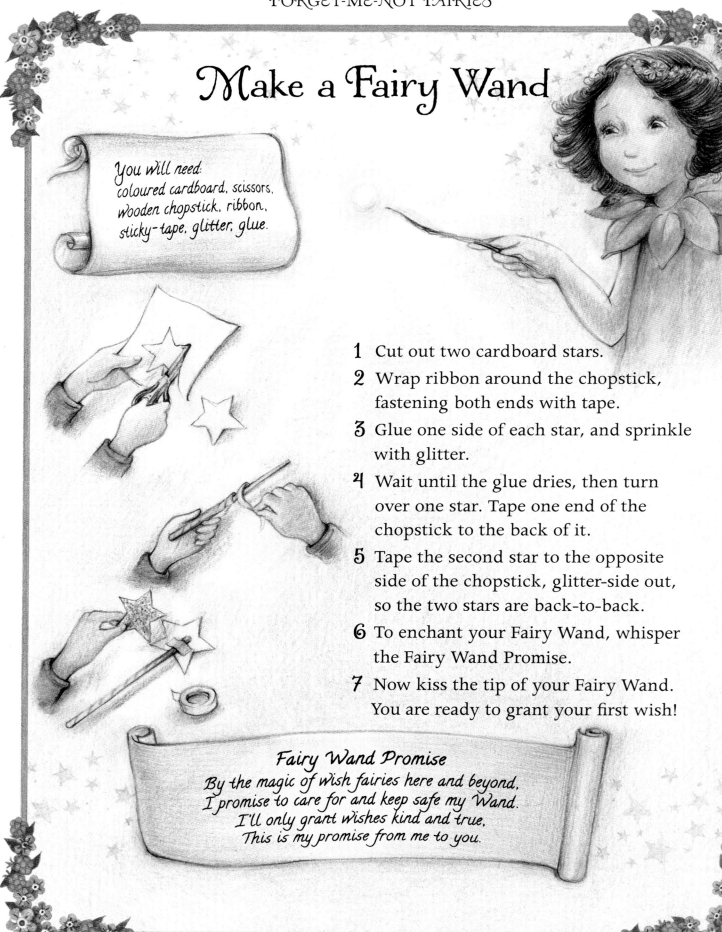

You will need:
coloured cardboard, scissors, wooden chopstick, ribbon, sticky-tape, glitter, glue.

1 Cut out two cardboard stars.

2 Wrap ribbon around the chopstick, fastening both ends with tape.

3 Glue one side of each star, and sprinkle with glitter.

4 Wait until the glue dries, then turn over one star. Tape one end of the chopstick to the back of it.

5 Tape the second star to the opposite side of the chopstick, glitter-side out, so the two stars are back-to-back.

6 To enchant your Fairy Wand, whisper the Fairy Wand Promise.

7 Now kiss the tip of your Fairy Wand. You are ready to grant your first wish!

Fairy Wand Promise
By the magic of wish fairies here and beyond,
I promise to care for and keep safe my Wand.
I'll only grant wishes kind and true,
This is my promise from me to you.

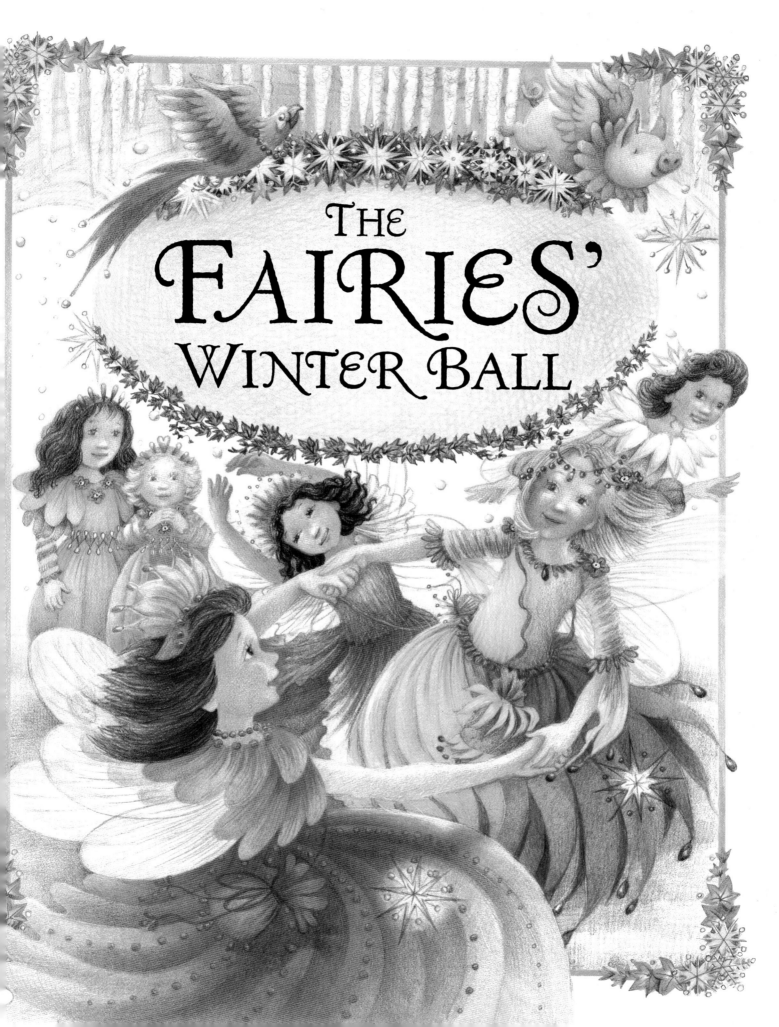

THE FAIRIES'
WINTER BALL

After a night of heavy snowfall, Ellen and Sophie awoke to the sound of tapping at their bedroom window. Willow was hovering just outside in the morning light. Two pairs of birds fluttered beside her, each pair carrying a box with a bow. Ellen leapt up and opened the latch to let them inside. The little group flew in, and Willow unrolled a scroll, from which she read:

'Miss Ellen and Miss Sophie,

Queen Flora invites you to attend the Forget-me-not Fairies' Winter Ball today. Please wear your gift.'

'A ball!' cried Ellen.

'A gift!' cried Sophie.

The fairy took fairy dust from her pouch and blew on it. The bow on each box untied itself by magic, and the boxes opened. Inside each was a pair of shoes.

Sophie stared at them and touched one shoe gently. 'They're made of ice!'

Ellen's eyes widened as she nervously slipped on a shoe. 'How strange!' she said. 'It's warm! But how?'

Willow smiled. 'Magic, of course!'

'Thank you for the invitation,' replied Ellen, grinning. 'We accept!'

'Then we shall see you at the ball,' said the fairy. With that, she and the birds flew off out of the open window.

After lunch, the sisters put on their best winter dresses and tiptoed out of the house in their new ice shoes. Unfortunately, Mama and the gardener, Thomas, were talking right in front of the archway to Wishaway Wood.

'What are we going to do now?' whispered Sophie.

'Psst!' said a voice from behind a bush. It was Bilberry the gnome wearing a bow tie and top hat. 'There's another way in, girls. Follow me.'

Bilberry led the sisters into the old greenhouse. It had not been looked after for years. 'I've never been to Wishaway Wood this way before,' he confessed, 'but I'm told we must look for a magic password.'

Sophie's ice shoes sparkled. She got the feeling they wanted her to go towards the back of the greenhouse. She walked over to a large flagstone with letters carved into it and stepped onto it. 'Over here!' she called.

Ellen and Bilberry came over and joined her on the flagstone. 'N-I-L-B-O-G,' Ellen spelt out. 'Nilbog?'

As soon as she uttered the word, the flagstone flipped sideways, and the trio went tumbling down a hole.

'Whooooooaaa!' cried Ellen as they slid down a tunnel.

'Wheeeeeeeeee!' cheered Sophie.

'Better watch out when we land,' called Bilberry, sliding behind them. '"Nilbog" is "goblin" spelt backwards.'

'Goblin!'

'Didn't I mention this is the goblins' entrance to Wishaway Wood?'

'No, Bilberry!' replied the girls. 'You didn't!'

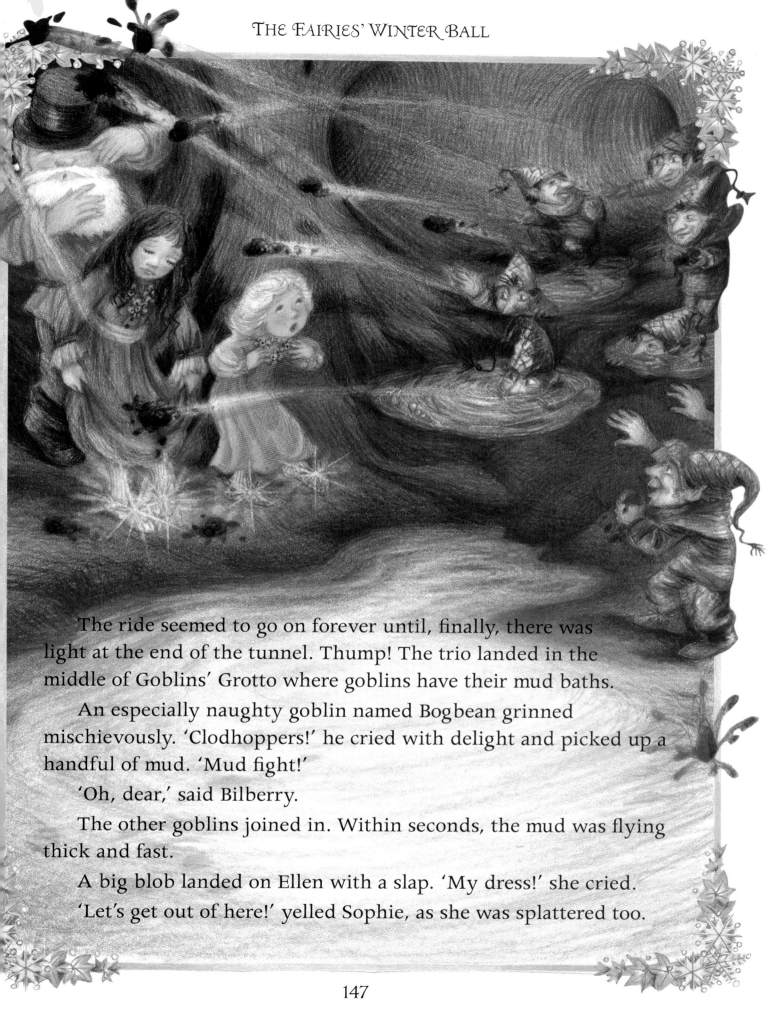

The ride seemed to go on forever until, finally, there was light at the end of the tunnel. Thump! The trio landed in the middle of Goblins' Grotto where goblins have their mud baths.

An especially naughty goblin named Bogbean grinned mischievously. 'Clodhoppers!' he cried with delight and picked up a handful of mud. 'Mud fight!'

'Oh, dear,' said Bilberry.

The other goblins joined in. Within seconds, the mud was flying thick and fast.

A big blob landed on Ellen with a slap. 'My dress!' she cried.

'Let's get out of here!' yelled Sophie, as she was splattered too.

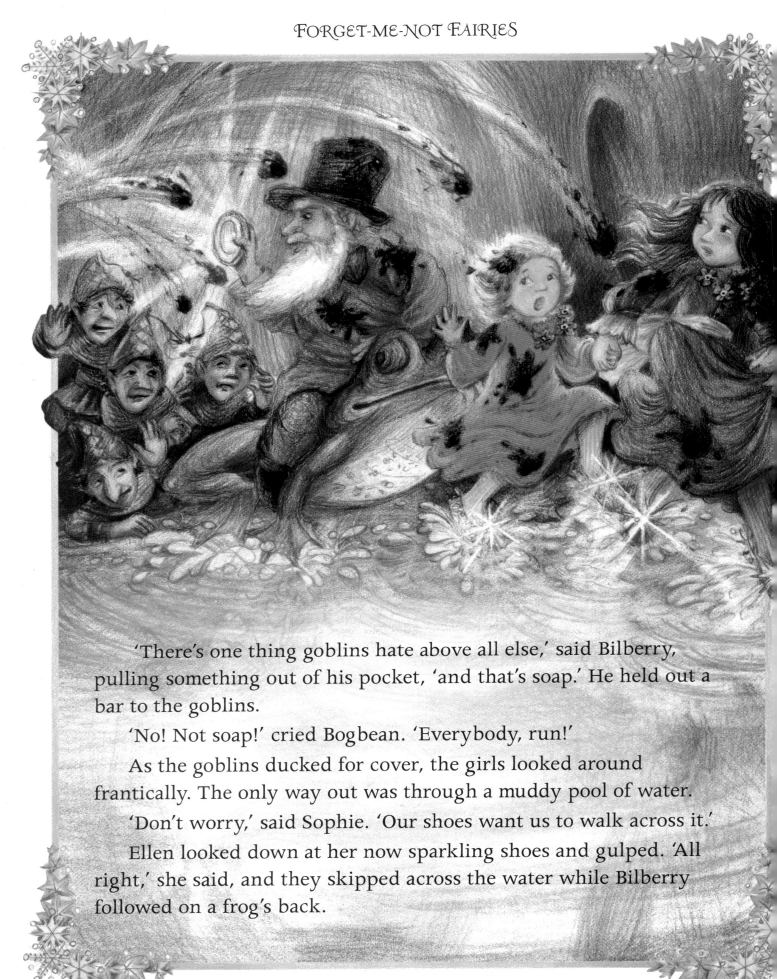

'There's one thing goblins hate above all else,' said Bilberry, pulling something out of his pocket, 'and that's soap.' He held out a bar to the goblins.

'No! Not soap!' cried Bogbean. 'Everybody, run!'

As the goblins ducked for cover, the girls looked around frantically. The only way out was through a muddy pool of water.

'Don't worry,' said Sophie. 'Our shoes want us to walk across it.'

Ellen looked down at her now sparkling shoes and gulped. 'All right,' she said, and they skipped across the water while Bilberry followed on a frog's back.

Covered from head to toe in mud, they went straight to Mrs Milkthistle.

'My petals!' said the fairy. 'You can't go to the ball looking like this!'

With the aid of the magic cupboard, Mrs Milkthistle dressed Bilberry in a fancy purple tuxedo and the girls in gowns made of petals stitched together with silvery cobwebs. Luckily, their ice shoes only needed a sprinkling of fairy dust to clean them.

'One more thing,' said Mrs Milkthistle. She brought out two sparkling tiaras made of frozen raindrops and placed them on the girls' heads. 'Lovely. And, now, it's my turn for a dress.' She opened the cupboard door and out flew a stream of ladybirds. 'Whoops!' she said. 'Let's try that again!'

After Mrs Milkthistle had found a suitable dress, the little group left her cottage. Dozens of carriages were lined up outside, ready to take the fairies to the ball.

'Over here!' called Zinny, waving to Sophie and Ellen. Zinny and her friends were in a carriage drawn by a squirrel. 'Come with us.'

Sophie and Ellen jumped into the carriage, while Mrs Milkthistle and Bilberry climbed into another. Just then, the fairy piper began to play a tune announcing it was time to go. They travelled through the forest to the Fairy Castle.

'Look!' said Sophie, when they arrived.

Icicles hung from the branches of the large tree, glowing by the light of a thousand fireflies. Snowmen stood at the entrance, tossing petals over the guests. When the girls stepped from their carriage, birds made of enchanted snow flew above them, making patterns in the air.

Zinny took the girls' hands and led them to the entrance. 'Ellen and Sophie,' she said, 'welcome to our winter ball!'

When the sisters stepped into the ballroom, they gasped. Fairies in beautiful costumes danced beneath a ceiling of swirling snow. Water fairies played tunes on the icicles accompanied by a cricket orchestra.

'Would you like a lollipop?' asked a brownie, holding out a bunch of snowflakes on sticks.

'Yes, thank you!' said the girls.

Sophie took a long lick. 'Mine tastes like toffee!' she said.

'And mine tastes like strawberries and cream!' replied Ellen.

Willow gracefully flew across the room to the girls. 'Queen Flora wishes to speak to you,' she announced.

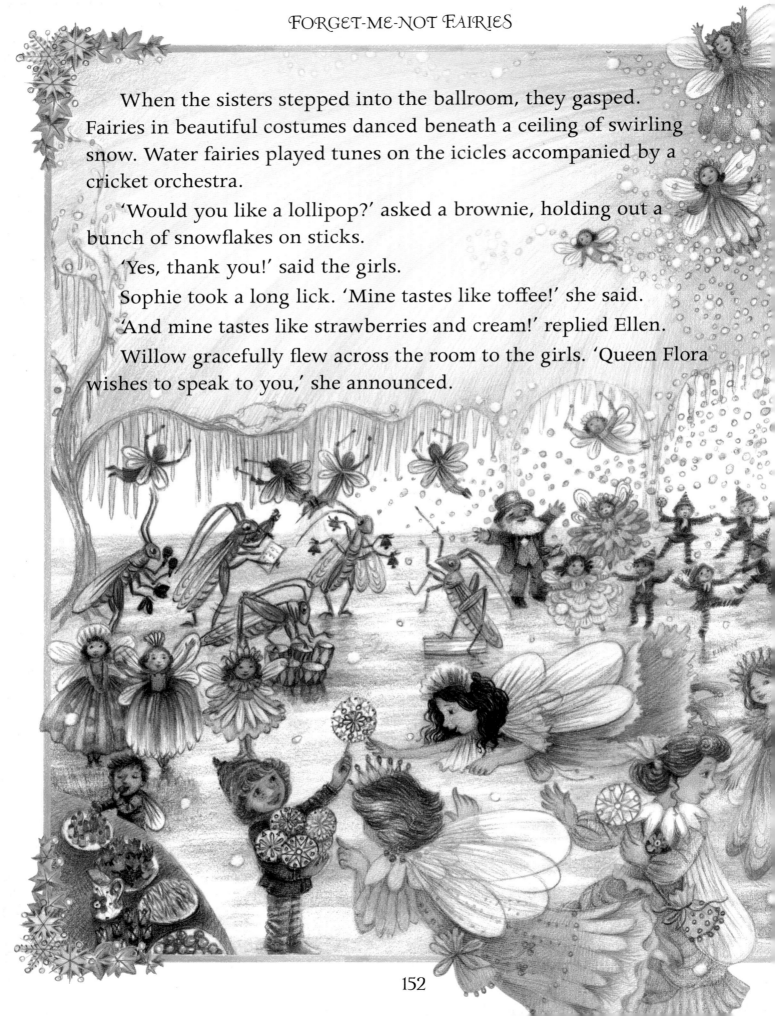

The sisters went over to the Fairy Queen and curtsied.

'Thank you for coming,' she said. 'You are the first clodhoppers ever to attend a fairy ball.'

'We're very honoured,' said Ellen.

'Yes,' said Sophie. 'It's wonderful.' She gazed around at the fairies waltzing on the ice floor. 'I wish I could dance like that.'

'But you can,' said Willow, nodding at their shoes. Ellen and Sophie looked down, and their shoes sparkled. A shiver ran through the sisters' feet, not of cold but of magic.

'Please go and enjoy yourselves,' said the queen.

Sophie and Ellen stepped onto the icy dance floor and glided across it as if they had been ice dancers all of their lives. As Sophie did a pirouette, her shoes lifted her into the air. 'I'm flying!' she cried, laughing with delight.

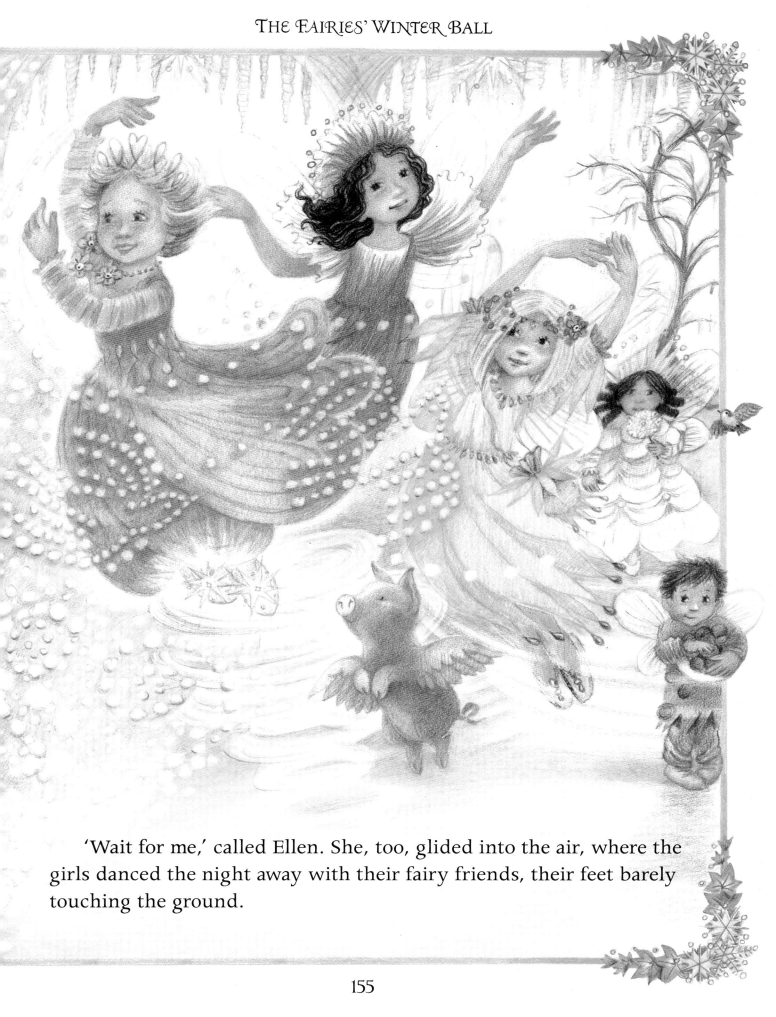

'Wait for me,' called Ellen. She, too, glided into the air, where the girls danced the night away with their fairy friends, their feet barely touching the ground.

The next morning, the girls awoke to the sound of Nora making breakfast downstairs. They rubbed their eyes and looked over at the dresser where, last night, they had left their enchanted ice shoes. But the shoes were gone!

'Was yesterday just a dream?' Sophie asked her sister.

The girls got up to look closely at the dresser. There, on top was a pool of water, the only proof they had ever been to a fairies' winter ball – that and their memories, of course!

Fairy Ball Gowns

Zinny

Poppy

Willow

Snowdrop

Play Wish Fairy Hopscotch

You will need: marker such as a coin or pebble, chalk.

1 Draw a hopscotch grid with chalk on the pavement or sidewalk.

2 Stand at the bottom of the grid and throw the marker into the first square.

3 Make a wish.

4 Hop over the first square and continue to hop in each square. Use two feet together whenever there are two squares side by side.

5 When you get to the end, turn around, still hopping, and come back. When you reach square two, pick up the marker in square one, then hop in square one and off the grid.

6 If you get through the grid without a mistake, your wish will be granted!

7 Start again, this time throwing the marker in square two. Play as before, but this time avoid hopping on square two. Do the same for square three, square four, and so on for each round.

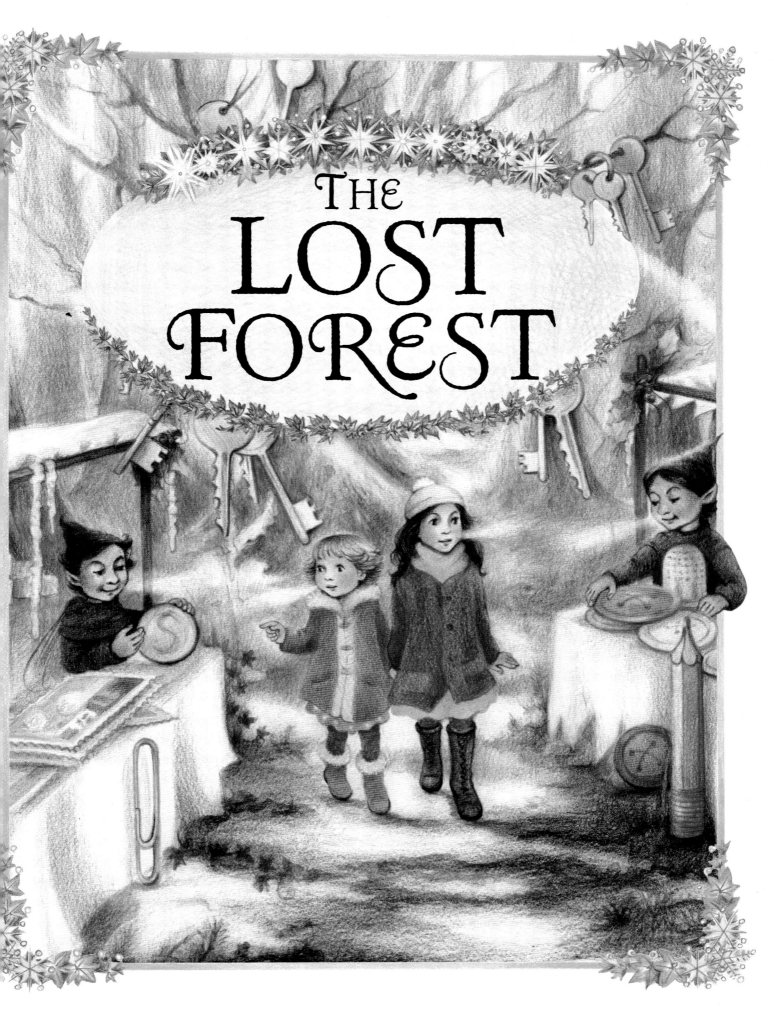

THE LOST FOREST

'Have you seen a pink button?' asked Sophie, hunting around in the hallway. 'That's the third one I've lost off my cardigan this month!'

'That's strange,' said Ellen. 'I've lost half my socks and my thimble is missing.'

The doorbell rang, and Sophie grinned. 'I bet I know who that is.' Great-Uncle Alfred was in town for a stamp collectors' meeting, and he was going to stay at their home. The girls had never met him before, but Papa said he was the funniest man in the world.

'Welcome!' said Ellen, opening the door.

'You're here!' cried Sophie.

A tall, thin man with a twirly moustache stood in the doorway. He looked the sisters up and down, and said, 'Please keep your voices down. I can't bear noisy children. They give me a headache.'

As Sophie and Ellen gaped at him, Mama came into the hallway. 'Do come in, Uncle Alfred,' she said. 'Once we've got you settled, I'm sure the girls would love to see your stamps.'

Great-Uncle Alfred frowned. 'Little children have grubby hands.'

He stomped up the stairs behind Mama, leaving Sophie and Ellen to stare at each other.

'I thought he was supposed to be the funniest man in the world,' said Ellen.

'More like the grumpiest,' muttered Sophie.

After lunch, Great-Uncle Alfred reluctantly agreed to let the girls look at his stamp album.

'I love that one,' said Ellen, pointing at a stamp of a bird of paradise. 'It's my favourite.'

'Such pretty colours,' said Sophie, reaching out to touch it.

'Hands behind backs!' commanded the old man.

The sisters jumped.

'Great-Uncle Alfred, when are you going to tell us a joke?' asked Sophie.

'Papa said you have a great sense of humour,' explained Ellen.

Great-Uncle Alfred snorted. 'I lost my sense of humour a long time ago,' he said gruffly, and he closed the stamp album with a snap.

The next morning, while the family were eating their breakfast, Great-Uncle Alfred stomped into the kitchen with a scowl on his face. 'Someone has taken my bird of paradise stamp,' he said, glaring at Sophie and Ellen. 'I am greatly displeased.'

'*We* didn't take it!' said Sophie.

'I'm sure it's just been mislaid,' said Mama. 'We'll look for it right away.'

While the grown-ups were hunting for the stamp, Ellen and Sophie got dressed. Soon after, Ellen noticed Pip, the water fairy, waving at her from the window. She let him inside.

'I was coming to say hello when I overheard your great-uncle. I think I know where the stamp is,' Pip said.

'Do you?' asked Sophie, hopefully. 'Where?'

'The Lost Forest,' said Pip. 'I can take you there, but you'll need to put on your boots first. You're going to get muddy.'

Sophie and Ellen looked at each other. Mud could only mean one thing – goblins.

Sophie scooped up Scampers. Together, the four of them made their way through the archway to Wishaway Wood. As the girls walked along, Pip hopped from icicle to icicle.

'Pixies like to "borrow" things from clodhoppers,' he said. 'Then they sell them to the goblins.'

'What sorts of things?' asked Ellen.

'Socks, keys, buttons ...' said Pip.

'Buttons!' cried Sophie. 'So that explains it!'

'Goblins love to decorate their caves,' said Pip. 'They're very houseproud.'

'They *are*?' asked Ellen, surprised. The last time she met a goblin, it involved a mud fight.

'Oh, yes,' said Pip. 'And they especially like stamps. They make lovely pictures for their walls, you see.'

The little group walked on until they heard a clinking sound. They looked up and saw dozens of keys hanging from a tree. 'Clodhopper keys!' said Pip. 'We've reached the Lost Forest.'

Just ahead, there was a market with all sorts of things for sale – buttons for use as plates, thimbles for bowls, socks for sleeping bags. One goblin was trying on a bottle cap for a hat. The girls stared in wonder.

'Let's find the stamp,' said Sophie.

'Yes,' said Ellen. 'Before a goblin buys it!'

167

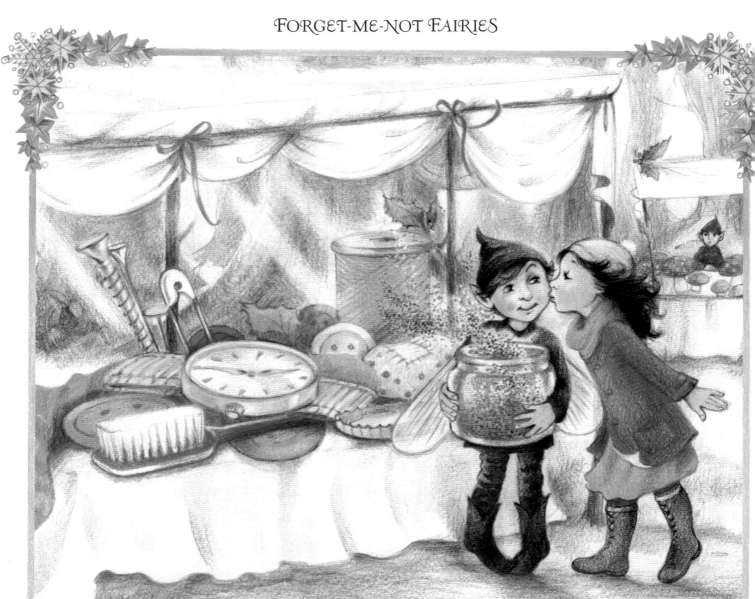

As the group wandered through the market, a pixie called out to them: 'Step right up and get your sense of humour here!'

Curious, Ellen went over while the others kept searching for the stamp.

'Clodhoppers are always losing their sense of humour,' said the pixie. He unscrewed the lid of a jar filled with purple powder. Ellen could just make out the sound of giggling.

'I don't have any money to buy it,' she said, sadly.

The pixie smiled. 'Just this once, you can have some for free.'

Ellen gave the pixie a kiss on the cheek and he tipped some powder into her handkerchief. 'It works best under a pillow,' he said.

While Scampers went off exploring, Sophie and Pip found the stamp stall. A goblin was holding up a bird of paradise stamp. 'I'll buy it,' said the goblin to the pixie behind the stall.

'No!' cried Sophie. 'That's my great-uncle's! Please give it to me.'

The pixie and goblin stared at her. 'A clodhopper in the Lost Forest! Well, I never!' said the pixie. 'If you can offer a better price, I'll sell it to you.'

The goblin held up a gold coin. Sophie had nothing. 'I could sing you a song,' she said, hopefully.

The pixie laughed and took the goblin's coin. 'Sorry, clodhopper.'

Sophie looked at Pip. They had to do something! But what?

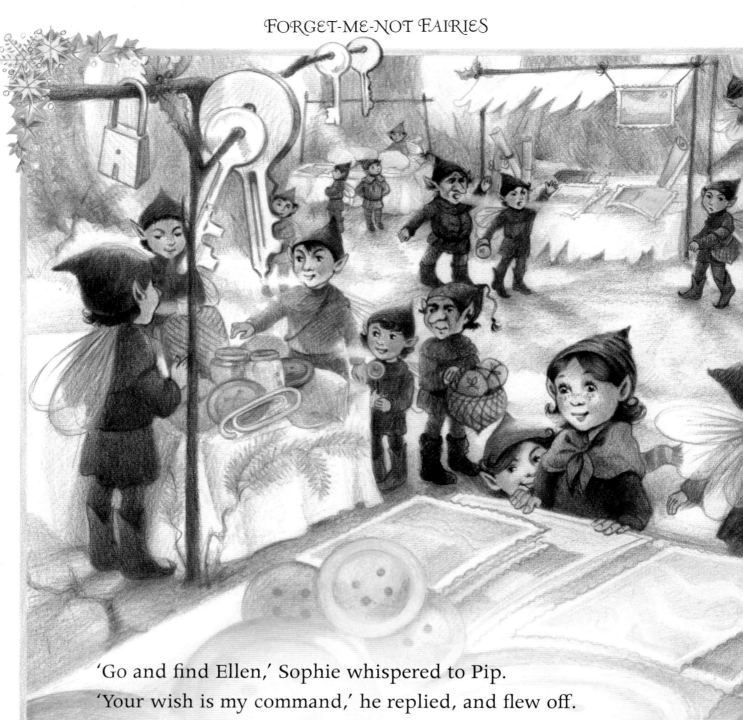

'Go and find Ellen,' Sophie whispered to Pip.

'Your wish is my command,' he replied, and flew off.

Meanwhile, Sophie whistled for Scampers. As soon as she saw the mouse coming, she turned to the goblin and the pixie. 'I'm terribly sorry,' she said, 'but that stamp belongs to someone else.' As soon as Scampers arrived, Sophie snatched the stamp, jumped on Scampers' back and took off.

'Come back!' yelled the pixie, shaking his fist.

'How will I decorate my living room now?!' shouted the goblin.

Sophie and the mouse raced through the crowded market. *Where are you, Ellen?* thought Sophie. As she looked around desperately, she spotted a tiny rainbow that Pip had conjured. Standing below it were Ellen and Pip.

'That way, Scampers!' she cried, and over they charged.

Ellen jumped on Scampers' back, and Pip flew up to an icy branch. 'Meet you back at your house,' he said, and disappeared into an icicle.

'Let's go, Scampers!' said Sophie, and they took off into the forest.

When they arrived back at home, the girls slipped inside and cleaned themselves up. Even Scampers got a bath, although he was not very happy about it.

Later, when the grown-ups had gone to bed, the girls crept out of their room and down the hall to Great-Uncle Alfred's bedroom. Ellen slowly turned the door handle and pushed. Creeeeeeeeeak went the door hinges. Sophie thought her heart might stop, but Great-Uncle Alfred slept on.

The two girls crept into his room where they found Pip peeking out of a vase, waiting for them. Sophie tiptoed over to the dresser and silently put down the bird of paradise stamp.

Meanwhile, Pip flew over to the bed and Ellen joined him. She took out her handkerchief filled with the purple powder from the market. The powder giggled softly in the dark. Ellen gave Pip a nod, and he lifted the corner of Great-Uncle Alfred's pillow. The old man was snoring so heavily that his snores ruffled Pip's wings. Ellen sprinkled the powder underneath the pillow. When she was done, Pip dived back into the vase and Ellen and Sophie slipped out of the room.

Now, all they had to do was wait and hope.

The next morning, Great-Uncle Alfred burst into the dining room. Ellen and Sophie looked up nervously from their porridge.

'I found my stamp!' he cried, excitedly. 'It's a miracle!' Great-Uncle Alfred did a little jig and then looked down at his clothes and blinked. 'What do you know! My pyjamas are on inside out! And, not only that, I'm wearing odd socks!' He roared with laughter. 'I'm sorry I was so bad-tempered before, girls. I don't know what was wrong with me. I say, would you like to hear a joke?'

'Yes, please!' said Ellen and Sophie, grinning.

It seemed Great-Uncle Alfred had found his sense of humour.

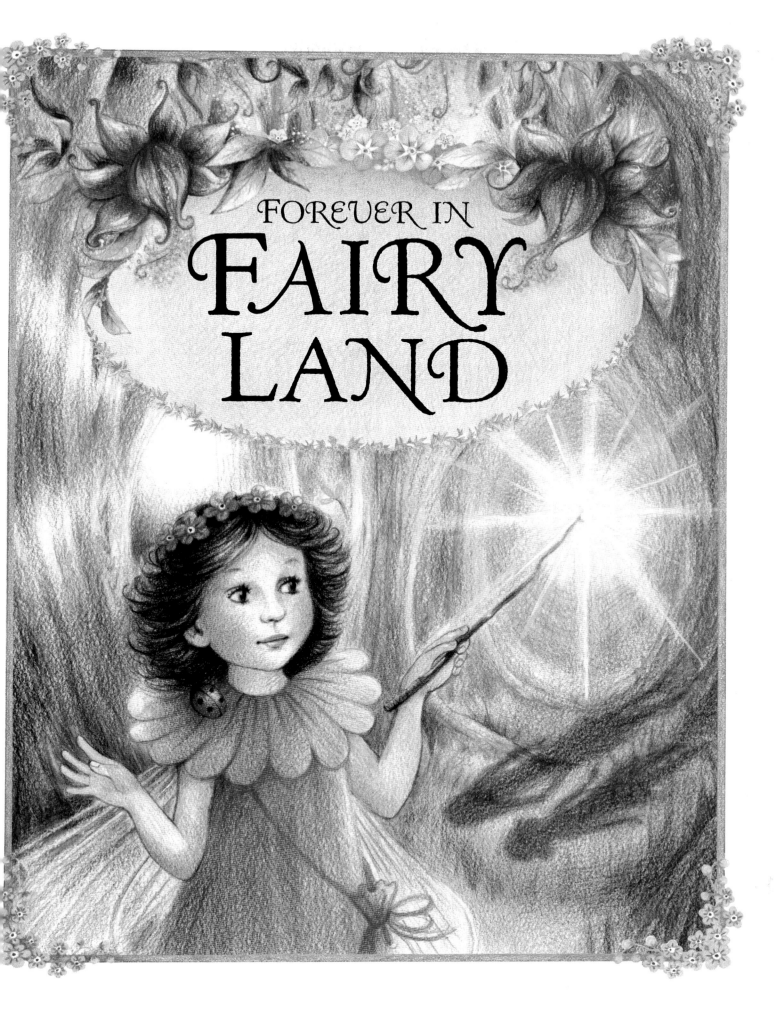

FOREVER IN
FAIRY
LAND

'Over here!' called Zinny, waving to Sophie and Ellen. The girls had been invited to Professor Fig's special wand class.

Sophie sat down on a spare toadstool.

'Ellen, you can share mine,' said Snowdrop, shyly.

Professor Fig cleared his throat. 'Today, we're learning how to levitate a blueberry,' he announced. 'Any volunteers?'

Zinny's hand shot up. 'I need all the practice I can get,' she whispered to the girls.

Sophie and Ellen nodded. Zinny's spells had a habit of going wonky.

'Please come forward,' said Professor Fig. He blew on some fairy dust, and a blueberry appeared in his hands. 'Now, point your wand at the berry.'

Zinny pointed her wand.

'Next, think about the berry lifting into the air.'

Zinny closed her eyes and did so.

'Finally, cast your spell,' finished the Professor.

Zinny crossed her fingers and concentrated. Everyone in the class leaned back. Snowdrop covered her eyes.

'Good luck!' called Sophie and Ellen.

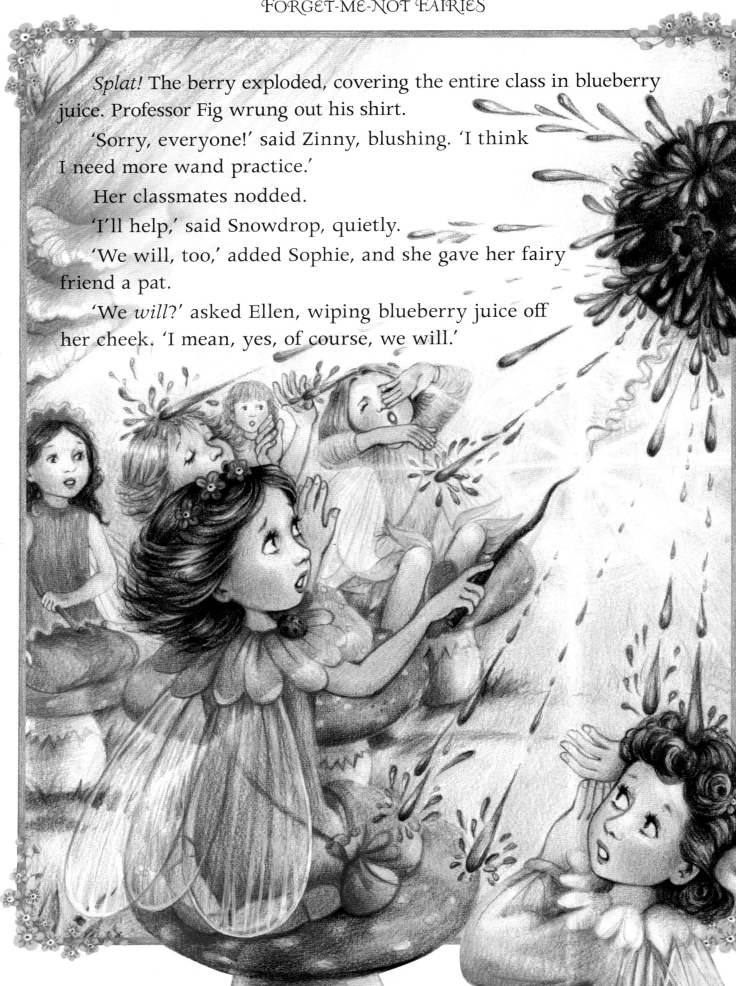

Splat! The berry exploded, covering the entire class in blueberry juice. Professor Fig wrung out his shirt.

'Sorry, everyone!' said Zinny, blushing. 'I think I need more wand practice.'

Her classmates nodded.

'I'll help,' said Snowdrop, quietly.

'We will, too,' added Sophie, and she gave her fairy friend a pat.

'We *will*?' asked Ellen, wiping blueberry juice off her cheek. 'I mean, yes, of course, we will.'

Wand practice took place that afternoon. Fortunately, time passed more quickly in Wishaway Wood, which meant the girls could stay for a long time without being missed at home.

'Let's separate a leaf from its shadow,' suggested Snowdrop.

Ellen found a leaf and placed it on a rock.

'You must find the magic within you,' explained Snowdrop to Zinny, 'and let it travel through your wand.'

Zinny felt a warm glow in her heart, and then sparkles shot out of the end of her wand. Everyone held their breath. The leaf's shadow slowly peeled away and danced around the leaf.

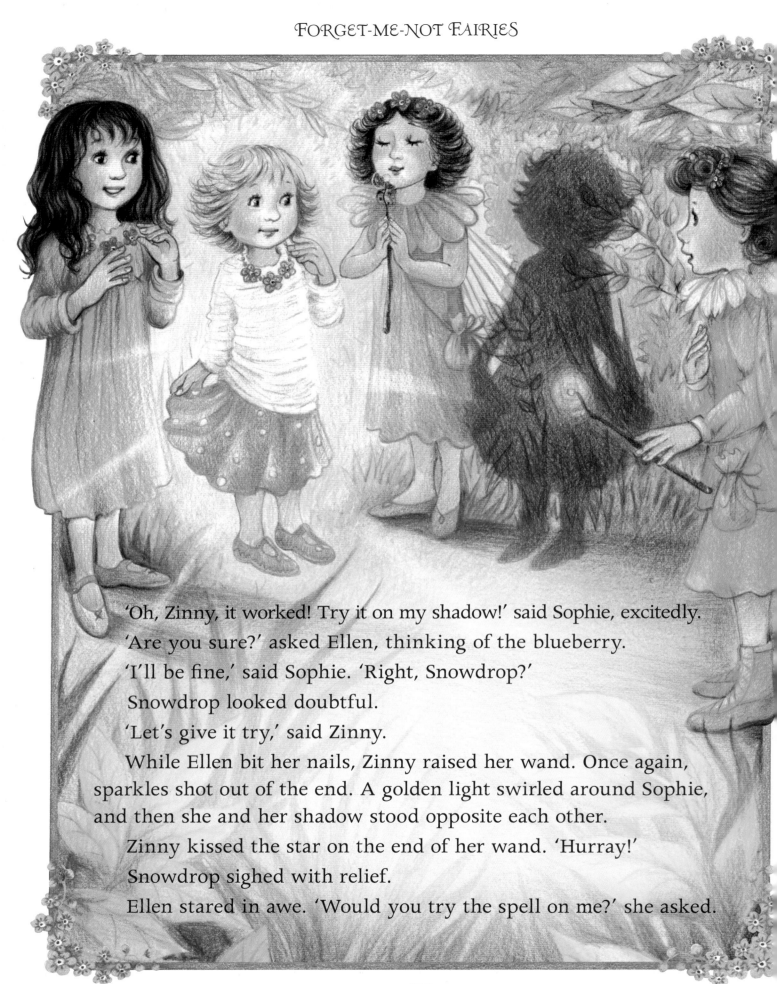

'Oh, Zinny, it worked! Try it on my shadow!' said Sophie, excitedly.

'Are you sure?' asked Ellen, thinking of the blueberry.

'I'll be fine,' said Sophie. 'Right, Snowdrop?'

Snowdrop looked doubtful.

'Let's give it try,' said Zinny.

While Ellen bit her nails, Zinny raised her wand. Once again, sparkles shot out of the end. A golden light swirled around Sophie, and then she and her shadow stood opposite each other.

Zinny kissed the star on the end of her wand. 'Hurray!'

Snowdrop sighed with relief.

Ellen stared in awe. 'Would you try the spell on me?' she asked.

A moment later, Zinny cast her spell, and Ellen also stood opposite her shadow. Then both girls took their shadows' hands and, together with the fairies, they danced in a circle.

After playing for much of the afternoon, Snowdrop had to go. Her job was to look after sick forest animals – removing thorns from paws and healing fevers. 'Bye for now,' she said.

'Time to reverse the spell,' said Zinny. But, when she raised her wand, the shadows, who had been enjoying their freedom, ran off into the woods.

'Uh oh,' said the girls.

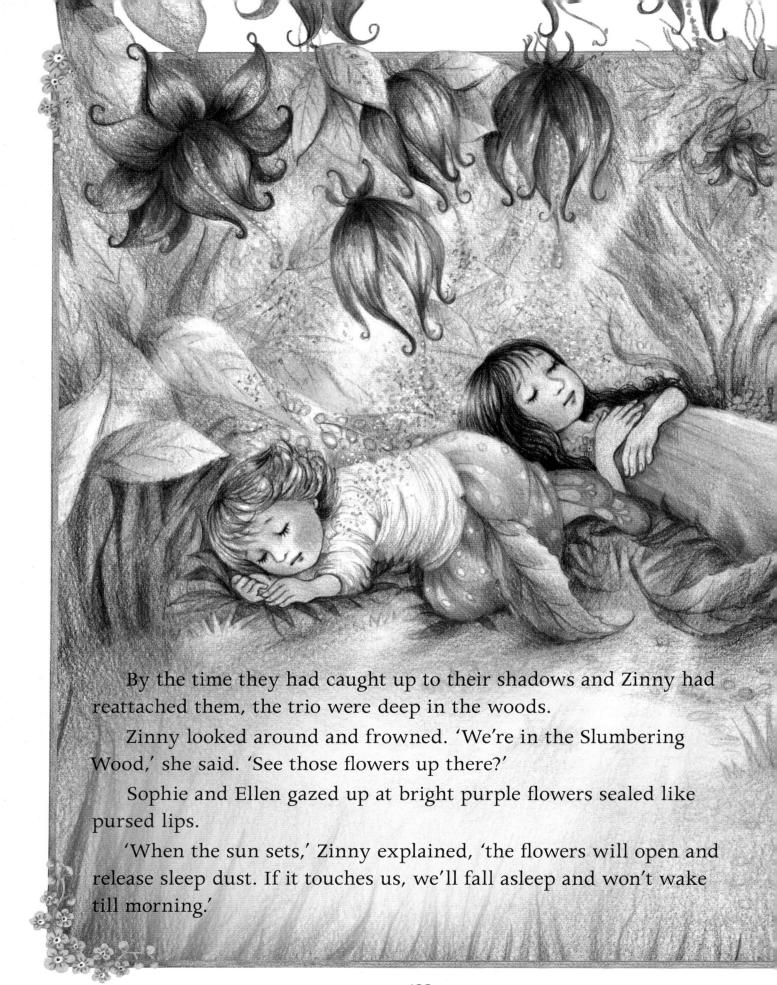

By the time they had caught up to their shadows and Zinny had reattached them, the trio were deep in the woods.

Zinny looked around and frowned. 'We're in the Slumbering Wood,' she said. 'See those flowers up there?'

Sophie and Ellen gazed up at bright purple flowers sealed like pursed lips.

'When the sun sets,' Zinny explained, 'the flowers will open and release sleep dust. If it touches us, we'll fall asleep and won't wake till morning.'

Ellen's eyes widened; the sun was beginning to set. 'But didn't the Fairy Queen say that if we stay in Wishaway Wood longer than one day and one night, we'll have to stay forever?'

Sophie gasped. 'We got here very early this morning, so ...'

'We need to leave very early tomorrow,' finished Ellen. 'We can't risk falling asleep here. We might sleep in! Let's go now!'

Zinny looked around, trying to work out which path to take. Above her, the petals of the purple flowers were starting to open. 'I think it's this way,' she said. But, when she heard no reply, she turned around. 'Sophie? Ellen?' Sleep dust was drifting gently down. The sisters were curled up on the mossy ground, fast asleep. 'Oh, no,' said Zinny, yawning. 'We're too la—zzzzzzzzz.'

When the sun rose the next morning, Zinny and the girls were still asleep. Luckily, when they had not returned, a worried Snowdrop had sent some squirrels and a rabbit to find them. The squirrels nudged the group with their noses.

Sophie woke first. 'Where am I?' she asked. Then she remembered. 'Wake up!' she cried, shaking Ellen and Zinny. 'We have to get to the archway before it's too late!'

The girls jumped on the rabbit's back and raced across Wishaway Wood, with Zinny flying just ahead.

As soon as they reached the gateway between the two worlds, Sophie jumped down. 'Thank you, Mrs Rabbit,' she said.

Ellen leapt off too and took Sophie's hand. 'Ready?'

Sophie nodded, and Zinny kissed them goodbye.

Then, the girls stepped forward. But, instead of going through the archway, they bounced back and fell onto the ground. The archway was sealed. They were trapped!

Zinny and the girls went straight to Mrs Milkthistle's cottage to see if she could help.

The wise old fairy shook her head with concern. 'The rules of Wishaway Wood have been in place since the beginning of time,' she said. 'They can't be changed.'

'No!' cried Sophie, clapping her hands over her mouth. She loved Wishaway Wood, but to stay here forever and never see Mama and Papa again? It was unthinkable!

'This is all my fault!' cried Zinny, flitting about the cottage. 'Isn't there anything you can do, Mrs Milkthistle?'

'Let me consult my spell book,' replied the fairy.

While Mrs Milkthistle flipped through her book, Ellen put her arm around Sophie and tried not to cry.

The older fairy hummed to herself as she peered at spell after spell. 'Well, what do you know?' she said. 'It says here that, if the moon is blue, anyone caught in the fairy kingdom may return home.'

Mrs Milkthistle got out her star chart. 'Look! For the first time in three years, there will be a blue moon tonight. The Spirit of Wishaway Wood has been good to us, petals.'

That night, the moon was as blue as blue. The fairies and the girls gathered at the Magic Ring of Toadstools. Sophie and Ellen stood in the middle, wondering if they would see their fairy friends again or if this was goodbye forever.

'Hold onto your forget-me-not chains, petals,' said Mrs Milkthistle. 'It's time to make your wish.'

The girls looked at each other, touched their chains, and whispered over and over, 'We wish to go home. We wish to go home.'

The fairies danced around the toadstools, singing a magic song:

'The moon is blue, the sky is clear,
Your wish is home, but you are here.
We circle toadstools three times three,
From Wishaway Wood, we set you free!'

Each of the fairies took a handful of fairy dust and blew it over the girls. As the magic surrounded them, Sophie and Ellen felt tingly all over. Then, their feet lifted into the air, and they began to spin. Around and around they went, clinging to each other as the stars swirled around them. Then they were falling, falling, falling until …

Thud! Ellen and Sophie landed on soft grass. They were dazed at first and were not sure where they were. Then they heard Nora, their housekeeper, singing as she hung out the washing.

'We're home!' cried Sophie, hugging her sister tightly.

'Yes,' said Ellen, sighing with relief. 'But will we ever be able to visit Wishaway Wood again?'

'Ahem,' said Bilberry, clearing his throat.

'Bilberry!' they cried. 'It's you!'

'Look!' said the gnome. 'The fairies have sent a message.'

The girls turned to find their garden covered in a carpet of forget-me-nots. Sophie and Ellen quickly felt around their necks – their chains were still there. The fairies had not forgotten them, and they had not forgotten the fairies! Sophie and Ellen smiled at each other. The flowers were a promise that they could visit Wishaway Wood again. All they had to do was step through the archway and believe.

Wish Fairy Lullaby

The stars are twinkling in the sky,
It's time to go to bed;
The birds are folding up their wings,
So rest your weary head.
Rest your weary head, my dear,
Beneath the moon's bright beams;
We fairies won't forget you,
For we'll see you in your dreams.
We'll see you in your dreams tonight,
We'll keep a watchful eye;
We'll sing to you until you sleep,
This fairy lullaby.

N

W   E

S

WISHAWAY WOOD.

The Lost Forest

Goblins' Grotto

underground tunnel

Clodhoppers' Greenhouse

Moonbeam Bridge

Make-a-Wish Mountains

Ladybird Lake

Magic Ring of Toadstools

Archway

Village Green

P.M.